UNLIKELY STORIES

An
anthology
of horror
and
comedy
stories

V. Subhash

Unlikely Stories

Written, illustrated & designed in 2022 by

V. Subhash
(www.VSubhash.in)

Copyright

© 2022 V. Subhash. All rights reserved.

First edition

Published by V. Subhash

ISBN (for paperback)

979-82-1554-775-5

Disclaimer

This book is a work of fiction. Any resemblance to real persons, ghosts, evil spirits or monsters is entirely coincidental and strictly unintentional.

Acknowledgements

All illustrations by V. Subhash except for images by artists from Pixabay.com: ★ Calzas (lady on the paperback cover) ★ Dina Dee (*Femme fatale*) ★ Inna Mykytas (*The swim* and *Family planning*) ★ Maxim Kalmikov (*The lift*) ★ Naidiz (Tower of Pisa) ★ Pexels (cover background photo) ★ Racheal Marie (*The trip*, *The exorcism*) ★ SilviaP_Design (skeleton on the cover, *The seance*, *The shapeshifter*, *The haunting*) ★ StockSnap (laptop and ghostly silhouette) ★ zizwix (*Alien encounter*)

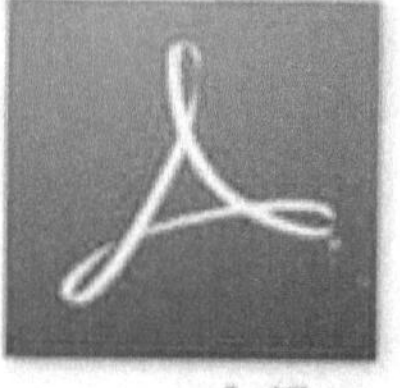

Free PDF samples of this and other books are available at

WWW.VSUBHASH.COM

Preface

I think I have read all kinds of fiction, except romantic fiction. Thanks to my school library, I had read almost every English classic novel that was abridged by S.E. Paces and published by *S. Chand & Sons*. After my 10th final exam, I became a member of a lending library in my hometown. The librarian introduced me to various genres of novels. He then asked me if I was interested in crime fiction. I did not want him to think that I was criminally inclined so I said no. He then showed me a rack with Enid Blyton and Carolyn Keene books. *Nancy Drew* mysteries (from the 80s) were difficult to lay my hands on in the school library but here they were so many of them without any competition. I began with *Nancy Drew*, moved on to *Hardy Boys*, and then to Enid Blyton's *Famous Five* and *Secret Seven*. One day, I found Erle Stanley Gardner among these books and became interested in crime fiction again. (I had already read a huge volume containing all Sherlock Holmes stories from the school library. I can also say I have read almost all short stories of Mark Twain and H. H. Munro (*Saki*), thanks to similar volumes of their complete works.) I then began reading Sidney Sheldon, Jeffrey Archer and some other high-demand authors. Their books were almost never on the shelves so one day I was looking for a new author. Then, I found a rack with James Hadley Chase books. In all his novels, there was a skimpily clad woman on the cover. There was no connection between the story and the cover. But, the covers sold tens of thousands of these books in India. My fiction books will try to imitate this style. As for what is between the covers, I am reminded of Robert Rankin who preferred not to follow the prevalent silliness and instead left a couple of pages blank for the reader's imagination (of exactly what you think). If I have to, in my fiction endeavours, I will do the same.

One day, I found a book in the school library that steered me towards non-fiction. I am not sure if it was *Up from slavery* by Booker T. Washington or *My experiments with truth* by MK Gandhi. Autobiographies had the drama that fiction books usually provided and the valuable information that non-fiction books usually provided. Eventually, I stopped reading fiction. The only fiction book that I had read in last two decades is the *Diary of a social butterfly* by Pakistani satirical columnist Moni Mohsin. It is a collection of her weekly articles in *The Friday Times* written around actual political events in Pakistan. I have followed her style in this book. No explanations to explain local stuff to foreigners. (Their guess is as good as mine.) A lot of Indian authors bend over backwards trying to cater to foreign readers. Their awkward explanations interrupt the flow and destroy the authenticity of the narration.

In 2020, I started publishing books and almost all of my titles were non-fiction. (There is one book of illustrated Aesop's fables whose endings I had changed with a humourous twist.) In 2022, I ran out of hobbies or interests to base my next book. Meanwhile, I had become a fan of 80s movies, particularly horror and comedy movies, from around the world. (The 80s seems to have been a decade of creative explosion in music and films.) Their politically incorrect laissez-faire approach to entertainment greatly appeals to me. Some of these horror movies gave me unusually vivid nightmares. For the next few days, I would try to recollect as much detail from the dreams. A few have made into this book.

The main story has two endings. The first one is that the lead pair live happily ever after. The second one is a parody of the controversy over *Men Writing Women*. Apparently, a lot of male authors have been corrupted by Japanese anime. That is what happens when a society eats too much soy.

I have also written into the main story some important information about health and well-being that young people need to be aware of before they embark on life's journey as an adult.

Like a good Indian masala film, this novel combines several genres — action, fantasy, supernatural/paranormal, sci-fi, contemporary, humour and horror. It will appeal to anyone anywhere above the age of 16.

What it does not have is content pandering to certain people who have short-changed their analytical ability with propaganda churned out by globalist kleptomaniacs. When creative individuals try to remain true to their beliefs, these people complain that they are being ignored. When some writer does include them in the storyline, they accuse the writers of of *writing about a group they did not belong to.* You can do nothing right by these Nazis. Because so many creators have chosen to just ignore them and avoid getting into any controversy, I think the globalists have chosen to browbeat all non-conformists with bad reviews. Several allegedly *authoritative voices* have been hired to amplify their harmful ideas and eliminate any diversity of thought. The effortlessly written attacks of these *nabobs of negativity* and their wannabes have destroyed innumerable movies and books. They have also ruined the creative ambitions of numerous actors, directors and authors.

Dead Sushi (2012) ★ 4/10

The Audience Loved It. Me....I Don't Get It

... I have to admit – I am not particularly a fan of outlandish Japanese films... Yet, I cannot deny that their cultish popularity. As the audience began amassing inside the theatre for the Toronto After Dark Festival screening of Noboru Igushi's Dead Sushi, the excitement was more palpable than for any other film in the very successful Festival in 2012.... The audience at the Toronto After Dark Film Festival knew exactly what they were about to revel in and they did so with an unwavering glee. They clapped, cheered and laughed ... We, well, we were mildly entertained more by the audience reaction than anything else. If the same film was given to us as a screener for home, we are not sure we would have gotten past the first few chapters of the DVD ... It would be hard for us to recommend this film to anyone...

Despite the fact that expensively made propaganda-laden movies have bombed spectacularly at the box office, the poisoning of books, movies, TV programs, advertisements and even award shows with propaganda continues unabated. I now regret having cheered Michael Moore at the Oscars when he complained that we live in 'fictitious times'. I am anti-war and I was happy that someone tried to wake up the American people. But, he set off a chain reaction... I am not sure. Even as early as 1994, award-show activism was parodied in the movie *Naked Gun 33 1/3: The Final Insult* starring Leslie Nielsen.

Racquel, so many go to bed hungry in this nation. Yet, cat food is full of tuna! I can't help but think each time I go to the zoo and see those porpoises, crammed into those tiny tanks, what a waste that is! Butcher half of them now! That's hundreds of pounds of dolphin meat that can be fed to our cats, freeing up that tuna for our nation's hungry.

[*A lone person claps and then tries hide himself in embarrassment. Priscilla Presley gestures to Nielsen to continue hamming.*]

There are so many cold, shivering… in the night so, I say, take those cats and skin them. Use them for… to keep hundreds warm.

Now, it is rampant. Hollywood stars have appointed themselves as this generation's unofficial philosophers. I find all new movies and TV shows from America idiotic. I cannot stand the people, the dialogue or the stories. It is just preaching and not entertainment. I now specifically seek out *bad movies* and old movies to find quality entertainment. Plenty of good movies continue to be made. They just do not have the budgets that the propaganda duds have. You will not find them at the top of artificially boosted rankings.

The humourless joyless purveyors of entertainment create an artificial wall between creators and their fans. To make this book unpalatable to such *social justice warriors*, I have added content that is extremely toxic to them in the chapter *Alien Encounter*. (I do have a pseudonym for my political cartoons and satirical stuff.) These pages add nothing to the story and you can skip them entirely. I have provided a warning on the cover clearly explaining what this book is not. If the wrong kind of reader reads it and then goes online to complain about it, I would have already extracted my pound of flesh.

V. Subhash
Kerala, INDIA
June 2022

Contents

In memoriam

Several sensitivity readers killed themselves while reviewing this book so it is dedicated to their memory. All other sensitivity readers should follow their sterling example.

The Trip

my friend got a new SUV. As he desperately wanted to prove its usefulness to his wife, he decided to take his family to some faraway beach resort. He invited me to accompany them during the weekend. I will be the fifth person inside the vehicle after the four from his family. Some friend of his wife worked at the resort and offered them a massive discount. My friend thought his new expensive ride could benefit from a long-distance test drive and decided to take up on the offer. I was doing nothing on the weekend except wash clothes so I didn't mind going with them.

"You will take care of the transport, the accommodation and the food?"

"I will."

"And, I'm not being set up for some elaborate sales pitch?"

"No. Why do you think I'm going to do that?"

"Well, your past history makes me suspicious. My father still complains about the teak units you sold him. The last time I spoke to him, he specifically told me not to have ANY relationship with you… not even speaking to you."

"Fine. No sales pitch."

"You are not in any financial mess, are you? Are you planning to borrow money from me?"

"Would I buy a new SUV if I had money problems?"

"A new SUV? I don't know, man. I don't know how many but lots of people have told me… they were just casually talking to someone… someone like you… who claimed to be very rich… but by the end of the day their kitchen was full of unbreakable plastic containers and they had to start sleeping on a magnetic bed! Are you sure this is not part of a multi-level marketing operation?"

"No!"

"Well, I will tell you at the outset that I DO NOT HAVE ANY MONEY. I don't want to you to be disappointed to learn that later. All my money is in stocks and tax-saving fixed deposits. Banks will not let anyone close such deposits before five years. I cannot sell the shares because the market is down."

This guy was my best friend in the last few years of school and a few years afterwards. I do not trust him. His family went through some serious financial and health problems while we were in school. My family also had financial problems but he started looking for a job much earlier than I did. When I was still studying, he was selling teak farm units, goat farm units, chits, real estate… anything else you can possibly imagine. He pitched these things to everyone else but me because he knew I would say no. Even though, I had chosen the science group, I was more financially savvy than my classmates who had chosen the commerce group… Actually, this was what I claimed then. The reality was that I used to read the business section of the newspaper every day. I was just more aware of what was actually happening in the financial world. Theoretically, I was weak until I did my graduation in business administration. Whatever the case, nobody sold snake-oil products to me!

One day, after I had left for my computer class, he came to my home — knowing fully well that I would not be there. He enquired if I was there and my father innocently fell into the trap of asking what he was doing. Before the talk was over, my father was poorer by two-and-half grand.

This guy is a born salesman. He can sell anything to anybody. It was not gift of gab or some actual sales/marketing talent that made him successful. He had some paranormal psychic power that he did not realize he had or could consciously control. Most people just lost their mental resistance to anything he said. Any traditional reserve or natural scepticism they would normally have just vanished when he spoke to them. They thought he was honest and did whatever he asked them. It was as if he cast a magic spell.

I have met just one more guy like him. This other guy was not psychic or anything. He had the gift of gab and real sales/marketing talent. My computer centre wanted to organize an annual cricket match, and he went and collected sponsorships of over one hundred grand from big brands like Pepsi and MRF!

I have not met anybody else like these two guys. The second guy left my life when I left the computer centre. The first guy came back when he moved to my city recently. Unfortunately, he was on the *other* side of the city. So, for six months, we had not met. Now, he wants to see me.

I have plenty of money in my bank account but I was not going to admit that to him. The market was down but only two of my shares were down. If I sold my entire portfolio today, I will be making several times the amount I had invested. I had written a book on investing in stocks. He had not shown any interest in any of my books. Now, I am thankful for it.

Besides, he had told one another friend of ours that I was the most careful person with money when compared to everyone else in our friends circle. This was because I did not spend much and I made sure that anyone who owed me money paid me back every rupee. Even if this was not always true, I decided to live up to their expectations... in my dealings with them, that is.

I am not paranoid about MLM. Several people had complained to me how they had lost a lot of money buying unwanted products. They said these MLM guys were impossible to get rid off. You had to buy their overpriced products or they would not go. Just a few months back, I was shopping at a supermarket and a well-dressed guy accosted me and tried to shake my hands. He said he had forgotten my name and promised to call me after he recalled it. I have had several people tell me about my living doppelgängers so I gave him my phone number like an idiot. Several weeks later, he called me and recalled our meeting. He then proceeded to ask me if I was interested in a richly rewarding lifestyle change or something like that. I asked him if it was about MLM and he confessed it was. End of conversation. I could not believe someone would go to such elaborate lengths to set up a sales pitch.

Anyway, my concerns about the trip were now alleviated and I was on my way to his home. This would be the first time I will be seeing his wife or his kids. I had attended his wedding. From that event, I remember a priest who had a two-wheeler vehicle without a license plate. But, for the life of me, I could not recall how his wife looked.

He asked me to be at his place by 7 but we did not leave until an hour late. We were also stuck in traffic for an hour. It was a Friday evening so half the people in the city were leaving for their home away from home. By the time we left the rush hour traffic, it was clear that we would not be hitting the bed before midnight.

My friend has two kids. A girl aged six and a boy aged seven.

They are studying in a good school and they seem smart... smarter than their father was when he was in school.

His wife was riding shotgun because the kids wanted to sit with me. I asked my friend about the car or jeep or whatever the thing it was. And, he said it was a 2-litre diesel and that it had four-wheel drive. Other than that, he knew nothing, not even the mileage. I think the mileage is very low and he did not have the courage to admit that before his wife.

I asked the kids what they wanted to do when they grew up. The boy said he wanted to be a star in some TV song competition and the girl said she wanted to be like some Youtuber. That's it, guys! There is no future. We are doomed as a species.

"That's it. We are doomed. Our species is doomed," I said.

"They are watching TV all the time. This is what they have in their heads now. They will grow out of it," his wife said hopefully.

"When we were kids, we saw movies and thought the doctors had it good. We all wanted to be doctors."

"Yes, doctors and engineers."

"There was of course some rare girl or boy who wanted to be an astronaut..."

"I want to be an astronaut," said the boy.

"I want to be an astronaut," said the girl.

"Now, you guys want to be astronauts?"

Both nodded.

"Do you know what astronauts eat? Hmm? Hmm?" I asked both of them.

Both shook their head.

"Food paste!"

Both kids screamed and their parents chuckled.

"In space, there is no gravity. So, you cannot prepare or eat food like you do on Earth. They put their food as a semi-solid paste in barrels and take them to space. When they get hungry they, they stick a tube in the barrel and suck on it."

"Yuck!"

"Eeew!"

"You think that is revolting? Wait till you hear how they get their water?”

“Oh, no!”

“Do you know where they get their water from?”

"Hey," I asked my friend, "do you know where they get their water?"

“I think you are going to say urine…”

“Just urine?”

“Noooooooo!” both kids screamed.

“They squeeze every ounce of water out of everything, not just urine, my friend!”

“Now, who wants to be an astronaut?”

The girl pursed her lips. The boy shook his head.

“You can be a doctor or an accountant…”

“I will be a doctor.”

“Me too.”

“Doctor, really? Sick people, diseases, wounds, pus, fever, blood, urine, vomit, crap…”

“I don’t want to be a doctor.”

“No-uh!”

“You can get into computers and invest the money you get from it in stocks.”

“I’m going to be a software engineer.”

“Me too.”

“Is it really true about the water?” my friend's wife asked.

“Yes, it is. What is even more disgusting is…”

“Here we go again,” my friend said.

“… is that after they have squeezed out all the moisture, they pack the remaining filth into plastic containers and throw them out.”

“Really?”

“I wonder if these containers are also emblazoned with the NASA logo. Maybe they have to write the current date on the label before they fling them out into space.”

“Imagine some aliens coming near our planet and finding these containers. What will they think of us?”

"No wonder we are alone in the universe."

"So, Americans are like us when they go to space? Keep the house clean and throw the garbage out into the streets."

"Exactly."

We were nearing the resort when we decided to ask for directions. We stopped at a small shop. It was very isolated and the place gave me the creeps. The shop was part of a larger house. There was no one at the counter. The door to the house was closed. Somewhere in the inner rooms, a man and a woman could be heard yelling at each other. Suddenly, there was a crash and then silence. I looked at my friend and he also seemed to have no idea what to do. I pressed the bell. There was no answer. I checked the freezer for icecream even though it was close to midnight. The freezer was locked. A man came out of the house after an interminable delay. We bought some drinks and then asked for directions to the resort. The man said we need to go along the road for another half hour before we will see a large signboard identifying the resort. The kids wanted to sleep and my friend's wife climbed on to the backseat. I rode shotgun.

After about twenty minutes, I asked, ""Did you notice something strange at that shop?"

"No, did you?"

"Do you think your kids are asleep?"

"Maybe." He turned and turned back, "Yeah, they are. What's with the shop?"

"Didn't you look in the freezer?"

"What was in the freezer?"

"The dead body!"

Both kids started screaming and their mother joined in too for some good measure. My friend braked.

"So, you guys were not really sleeping, were you? I didn't think so."

The boy scowled and the girl tried to hit at me.

"I think we have reached the resort. We need to check in and find our rooms."

At the check-in, my friend wrote all our names and that of another person. I asked him who it was and he said another one of his wife's friends will be joining us tomorrow.

"How come your wife still has so many friends?"

"Why not?"

"Don't they know she is married to you?"

"What's wrong with me?"

"Wrong with you?"

"Yeah, what is wrong with me?"

"Have you forgotten the love letters?"

"What love letters?"

"Yes, what love letters?"

This was his wife. She came out of nowhere!

"I have published some love letters in my book."

"You wrote a jokebook and there is no love in it. The breakup jokes were titled as 'romantic jokes'."

I used to read Moni Mohsin's *Diary of a social butterfly* when I travelled. Each story in the book was self-contained. It did not matter how many times I read them, they always seemed fresh. Now, I read my own book. It is one of the biggest jokebooks of all time. Whatever chapter or page I randomly pick to read during my travels, it always seems fresh. I never lose an opportunity to make someone read the book. I picked out a page and pointed where she had to read. She shook her head, exhaled and started reading loudly.

Billet-doux

Darling,

Most worthy of your estimation after a long consideration and much meditation, I have a strong inclination to become your relation. As for my education and qualification it is not exaggeration or fabrication that I have passed matriculation with very little preparation. What do you say to the solemnisation of our marriage celebration according to the regulations, to the glorification of the modern civilization…

"I don't think this is what you were talking about."

"Of course, not. I never lose a chance to make others read my book."

"What is this 'love letters' about? Tell me. Tell the truth."

"What are you afraid about? You have two kids. He is condemned for life. You still don't trust him? If he does something wrong, I will break his bones and then tell you. You are like my sister. You have nothing to be afraid of."

"I hope so… brother," she said sarcastically and prepared to leave.

My friend picked up the remaining bags and started to leave too. At the door, he turned and said, "I will kill you tomorrow."

"See if you live today."

When I was a kid, we used to have a cat. On some mornings, it used to sleep on my chest. The cat is a tiny animal and its heart beats really fast. It sounds almost like a motor. In my dreams, I would start hearing this sound. I would believe that it was my own heart was making this noise. The sound would start slowly, pick up pace and maintain to a steady hum. I would then panic and open my eyes. It was then I would find that it was our cat was making this sound, not my heart. Whenever this happened, it was a terrible experience. The cat looked like it was meditating, not sleeping. Its posture was that of the Egyptian Sphinx. The only difference was that our cat's eyes were closed.

I had a similar experience today. It was not a cat but the kids. They were sitting on the bed next to me and waiting for me get up. When I opened my eyes, I saw two heads silently watching me sleep.

Usually, I get up before daybreak. But, today, because of the late arrival, I slept past my internal alarm. I asked the kids what they were doing there and they wanted me to tell a scary story like I did the previous night. I told the kids I needed an hour to freshen up and take breakfast. I told them I am not telling any stories on an empty stomach and asked them to scram.

The cottage was on the beach but quite some distance from the beach, almost a kilometre. It had a kitchen but we were going to take the meals at the check-in place, which also had a grocery store and a restaurant. This place served several other seaside cottages in the resort.

My friend and his family had already had their breakfast. I showered, changed clothes and went to the restaurant. When my friend saw that I was up, he left his kids with me. He and his wife were going to a nearby railway station to pick up the *other woman.*

I had a masala dosa, a pongal and a vada-sambar because I was past my usual breakfast time and very hungry. Then, I took a coffee and started to read the newspaper. The kids did not let me read though. They were fighting with each other and damaging the resort property. I had to get them out.

"Come on, kids. Let's go to the beach."

At the beach, I surveyed the scene. There were a few fishing boats from nearby villages on the far sea but none on the shore. The coast was clear. We had come in the off-season. There was a big but lonely tree on the beach with a lot of shade under it. I thought that if we brought some furniture from the cottage lawn, we could spend all day under the tree, so close to the beach, rather than holed up inside the cottage. I told the kids of my plan. They were excited about it and we set about to find some chairs.

At the cottage, we found some lightweight foldable chaise lounges. I picked two and the kids picked one. I had to carry all three chairs because the kids became tired in no time. I spent some time stabilizing the lounge chairs. After that, the kids were having fun on their own. After half an hour, the boy wanted to go for a swim and I wanted to wait till it was noon. I just wanted to lie there and read my book. I went back to the cottage and got my book. I read maybe one line and almost immediately fell asleep.

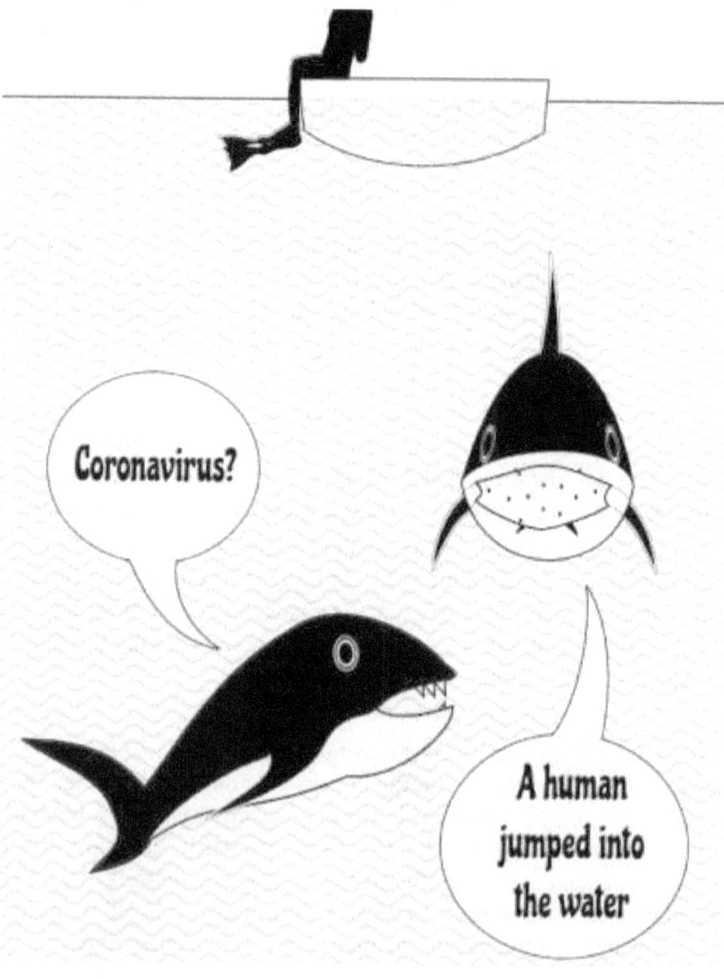

I must have been out for hours because the Sun was almost in the middle of the sky when I woke up. The kids seemed to have returned to the cottage. I went for a swim alone and returned to the cottage for a shower. I went to the kitchen to see if the kids had returned safely. There, everyone including the new girl and the kids were eating some kind of fruit. My friend's wife introduced me to her and said I was also a writer. I went through the 'oh really', 'no, not really' and 'don't be modest' routine for the nth time in my sorry life.

On the way back from the station, they had bought a jackfruit. My friend had cut it open with some difficulty but now everyone was eating the fruit. Their stock was already running low and I did not eat what they offered. I took the other half of the jackfruit outside. I said there was no room at the kitchen table and I did not want the knife to slip. My real reason was more selfish. Before you cut a jackfruit, you need to rub some edible oil on your hands and the knife. Otherwise, the sticky sap in the centre of the jackfruit will stick to the knife and make it difficult to cut into the fruit. The sticky sap will also stick to your fingers and anything you touch. Oil eliminates the problem. Besides that, a jackfruit releases strong odours, which are difficult to get rid off. After discretely applying the oil on my hands and a knife, I took the remainder of the jackfruit outside. I started removing the lobes from the jackfruit for my own exclusive consumption. I was not going to eat them now. I wanted to take them at lunch and later on the beach.

My friend accompanied me after a while. The kids had mentioned about the chaise lounges and the women went to inspect them.

"So, do you like the werewolf?"

"What wolf?" as I cut through the jackfruit.

"My wife's friend."

"Why do you say she is a wolf?"

"Didn't you see her teeth?"

"What teeth?"

"She had dental surgery to make them look like fangs."

"I didn't see it."

"She also had full-body tattoos. She used a laser procedure to remove them. You can still see them if you look closely."

"Did you look closely?"

"I did."

"I will ask your wife about that."

"The tattoos?"

"How closely you looked."

"So, what do you think about her?"

"I don't know. She seems all right to me."

"Not like a werewolf?"

"What's wrong with you? Since when do we make fun of beautiful girls? You have changed after you got married."

"You think she is still beautiful?"

"Maybe. Maybe not. Why are you so interested? Did your wife put you on this errand?"

"No!" he claimed and left. A few minutes later, he sent his kids to be with me. I went to lunch with them. I'm stuck with the kids now. How did I become their nanny?

After we finished lunch, we went to the beach again. My friend and the women were relaxing on our chairs but they left immediately for lunch after we joined them. I was eating from my fruit stash when my friend's wife came to take away the kids. It was their post-lunch nap time.

I was all set to have a nap myself when I sensed that I was being observed by somebody. I looked around and Vampira had materialized near me.

"Hi! Can I join you?"

"Sure," I said pointing to the empty lounge chairs.

The Swim

Vampira spent some time in the waters. She is thin. In my book, that's healthy. After her swim, Vampira went to the cottage for a shower. I took this opportunity to meet my friend's wife without Vampira being around.

"Your friend…"

"Do you like her?"

"I like all women."

"It's the women who don't like him."

"You want me to elaborate on the love-letter situation?" I asked her idiotic husband.

I turned back to her. "How come you are married and she is still single?"

"I got married immediately after I finished my exams. From the day I turned 18, my parents were warning that the a girl's youth had a limited shelf life and that I was going to get old like milk. Even before I got my certificate, they had tied this guy to my neck."

"Why did she get the teeth and the tattoos?"

"Her parents indulged her whims and fancies. There was nobody to tell her to stop and think. By the time she came to her senses, her appearance had completely changed. She looked like a vampire. Her parents are loaded so for the last few years they were also paying for getting the tattoos removed. She says she is not going to do anything to her teeth though. She still likes them."

"That's all I want to know."

My friend followed me out.

"So, the werewolf is not your thing, huh?"

"She might be my future missus so be respectful of her."

My friend almost sat down on the hot concrete and started laughing.

"I thought you might be interested in her but I never thought you will be thinking of marrying her."

I didn't say anything.

"So, in future, when we… normal people will be shopping at a grocery store, you will be getting half of your supplies from a pet shop!"

I waved a finger at him.

"If we have leftovers, can we give you a doggie-bag?"

I aimed a punch at him. "Stop it!"

"You know if you startle her or step on her tail, she might bite you with those teeth. Doctor will have to give you several painful shots around the navel."

Now, I punched him in the belly. He gasped for air and fell down. The concrete was hot and he tried to get up but could not. I grabbed his hand and stood him up. He still could not breathe. I slapped his back a few times and he seemed to recover.

When he got better, he said, "You are already frothing at the mouth. Let's go to a doctor and get this checked out. It could be serious."

"I'm going to put YOU in a serious condition."

"Don't get hot under the collar. Let me see if there are any puncture wounds around you neck."

He tried to inspect my neck. I brushed off his hand.

"Let us go to the beach and see if you are hydrophobic. So far, you don't seem to have any problem with the Sun. Let's see how you react to the full moon."

Then, he knelt on the ground, raised his hands like a dog and started howling. Somebody, get this guy a straightjacket. He has totally flipped.

I took out my phone, dialled a number, and said, "Hello, forest department? Water buffalo division, please. We have a wild animal on the loose here. Can you help us?"

"Okay. I will stop."

"Any time."

When we reached the lounge chairs, everyone else was already there. The kids hurrahed and dragged Vampira to us.

"They want to get into the water."

I took off my shirt and gave it to my friend. He went back to the tree where his wife was waiting. I took hold of the boy's hand and Vampira took hold of the girl's hand and we hit the surf. For a while, we were throwing the kids like they were volleyballs. When one of the kids remained under water longer than usual, we decided it was not safe and waded out of the waters.

My friend and his wife had already gone back to the cottage. They had placed a dry towel on each chair. My fruit stash was still there but the kids were depleting it faster than I liked.

"Were you two very close friends in school?"

"Not all the time. We studied in the same school from kindergarten. It was only in 11th when we both chose the pure-science group and got to study in the same section. We became close only after that. In the last year of our graduation, he moved to another part of city. We went our separate ways and did not have much contact until now."

"My friend says you both still fight with each other, like you did when you were in school."

"We are friends and we try to drag each other down however we can."

"My friend says her husband says you are jealous of him."

"He is jealous of me and I'm jealous of him. And, we take great pleasure in each other's failures."

She laughed and said, "It seems unusual."

"It is not real jealousy but we bully each other. Sometimes, our failures come in very handy."

"Really?"

"Maybe not. Looking back, maybe there is real jealousy. You see I'm the really good-looking guy and several girls were giving him love letters. I could not believe it."

Vampira laughed.

"He was really goofy-looking and then there were these reports of girls falling for him. He himself said he had received love letters. I could not believe it. Why someone in their right mind would go and give someone goofy-looking like him a love letter was beyond my understanding."

More laughter. The kids were intently listening but not laughing.

"Do you kids have to sit so close?"

They did not budge.

"Come on, let's go for a walk. I will explain what happened. It is beyond unbelievable."

I told the kids to maintain some distance between them and us.

"For several years, I did not believe it. In the beginning of our working careers, we were temping at a company. One day, two other girls joined us."

By now, the kids had closed the gap and were walking alongside our shadows. I gestured to Vampira sit down on the sand. I then asked the kids to kick their balls into the water and catch them when they return. This seemed to be an interesting exercise and the kids left us alone for some time.

My friend has an inferiority complex because he has dark skin. One day, he came to my house very depressed and complained that he had lost an interview because he was black.

"Did they give the job to a girl?"

"No"

"So, a guy got it?"

"Yes."

"Who cares about a guy's colour?"

"This is a sales/marketing position and they always give it to white guys. It is PARTIALITY!"

"They will give the job to whoever they think is going to make the biggest sales for them. Their salaries depend on that. Maybe the guy already has some experience or is better qualified. It is just a coincidence that he was white. You have not even finished graduation. You do not have experience, other than selling fraud financial products. They did not give you the job because you are stupid."

"I don't think so."

"Where there other white guys who were not selected? Did all white candidates get selected? You got rejected because you are stupid."

"So, that might really be the case? I'm stupid?"

"100%! At the start of our careers, we can be stupid. We will get experience over time. Everyone has to start from zero."

"Really?"

"I'm not stupid. Even I make big blunders. Let me give you an example. You remember our English teacher?"

"They guy who used to beat everyone?"

"Yeah. One day, while revising for the exams with one of our friends, I found something really stupid that I had written in my classwork notebook. In the lesson 'To Sir With Love', there was a question, 'Why was Mr. Braithwaite unemployed for 18 months?'"

"Yeah?"

"I wrote, 'Mr. Braithwaite was unemployed because he was a Black for 18 months.'"

My friend started laughing.

"Can you imagine what would have happened if the teacher had spotted it?"

"Oh, no! Stop!"

"He would have pasted the page on the notice board and converted it to a shrine. Everyone morning he would have gone there and done pooja for it."

"This is the funniest thing I have ever heard."

Finally, he got his cheer back. When he got on his cycle and prepared to leave, he loudly recalled, "'Because he was a Black for 18 months'". He shook his head, "Nobody can be that stupid!"

Vampira has been laughing uncontrollably for some time. The kids came back to see what the commotion was and there was no way they were going to leave us alone now. We walked back to the tree. My friend and his wife had returned.

"Where did you go?"

"Take your kids back. They are bugging us."

They grabbed their kids and went for an early dinner.

We remained on the chairs because it was not dark yet.

"After we had been working in a finance company for a few days, two girls had joined us for the same kind of work. One was good-looking like me and other was goofy-looking like my friend."

"Here we go again."

"Now, I realized that girls did give him letters but they were also ugly and stupid like him."

"Jealousy and spite."

"No, I accepted it was a case of you know Koundamani's 'ஏழைக்கு ஏத்த எள்ளுருண்டை' but his success with women made me wonder why I didn't even attract an average-looking medium-IQ girl to do the same!"

More laughter.

"Back at this company, I was busy checking some papers while the two goofs were talking. When I switched my attention back to their conversation, she was asking if she can send him a greeting card for his birthday!"

"Really? That fast?"

"Later, I asked him what made her say something like that on their first meeting. He says she had asked him his birthplace, mother tongue, religion, caste, sub-caste, sub-sub caste and so on. When she realized that they both belonged to the same community, she popped the birthday question. I never seen anyone lacking self-awareness so much than that day. It was only then that I realized my friend had some paranormal psychic effect on people. It was not limited to women. Everyone fell for him."

"It IS strange for someone to have an effect like that."

"Not on everyone but most people. I certainly don't think your friend married him for his looks or his magic charms. She is too smart for that. It was a stroke of luck for him that they chose him to get her married to. Anyway, from that episode, it became clear to me that women were not giving me love letters because they were normal and I was normal. My friend, on the other hand, is a telepathic extraterrestrial wearing a human skin."

"That I don't believe. Hypnotic powers, fine. Alien, no."

"What alien?"

The kids were back. They were soon joined by their mother.

"I'm sorry. They had dinner and just ran away."

"It doesn't matter. Sit down anyway."

"Tell us a scary alien story."

Their mother shushed them into silence.

"I have had another friend who had some sort of mind-reading ability. Would you like to hear about it?"

"Sure."

"One day, in our school, all classes were cancelled because all the teachers were engaged in preparing for the annual day or sports day or something. We were left to our own devices. The kids formed *ad hoc* groups to entertain themselves. In one group, a guy was demonstrating his 'telepathic' powers. His partner would ask a volunteer to secretly pick a page from a book. Then, in front of everyone, the partner would turn the pages of the book from the beginning and for each page he would ask 'Is this the page? Is this the page?' to the telepathic guy. When he came to the page that the volunteer had picked, the telepathic guy will somehow correctly answer, 'Yes, this is the page'."

"How did he do it?"

"It was very simple. When this stunt was repeated a second time, I noticed that the partner discreetly press his shoe against the shoe of the telepathic guy to signal that the correct page had been reached."

"I should have known that."

"I thought it was a neat trick and went to another group and secretly told one of the kids about this new trick. We partnered and were able to fool several kids in the same way. Inevitably, the kids became suspicious. One of them inserted himself between me and my partner. I pretended to take on the challenge as usual. On the first time after the conditions were changed, I leaned back on the bench when the correct page was reached. My friend caught on to that and said that was the page. Next time, I pressed really hard on the page. My friend correctly guessed that page too. Next time, I uncrossed my legs. Again, he spotted the signal and correctly identified the page. This went on for a while until I got bored. Somehow, my friend was able to correctly able to read my mind. I have no explanation how he did that. Then, he demonstrated a trick of his own. He asked me to write a word on his back with a finger and he would correctly identify it. I wrote the name of the girl who was targeting him at that time and he correctly guessed it. I thought this was a fluke and wrote several other words. He guessed all of them correctly. I asked him to write words on my back and I could guess nothing right."

"Why don't you write something on my back and let me guess?"

"Okay. Turn around."

"I think you wrote 'I love' or something."

"No, I wrote 'hello'."

We were both embarrassed. Fortunately, the kids jumped in and asked me to write on their backs.

"Your backs are too small to write. I have another trick you might like."

"No, try it."

"Write on my back." Both had their backs to me.

"Forget it. Just sit down both of you. This other trick is better. I call it the *phantom fingers trick*. You need close your eyes and stretch out your forearm to her like this," I told the boy. Then, I turned to the girl, "And, you place your index and middle finger here on his inner arm like this. Then, walk your fingers towards this position." I pointed to the skin crease between upper arm and forearm. I turned to the boy again and said, "And, when her fingers reach this place, you tell, 'Stop'."

The girl walked her fingers up his arm and about half-way up he claimed she had reached the target. When he opened his eyes, he was surprised.

"Once more! Once more!" he pleaded with her.

This time, he waited a little longer but he again opened his eyes prematurely.

Now, she said to him, "Do my hand."

Vampira was doing the same to her friend and later vice versa.

All of them were surprised at the result. Why! How! What! I had no answers.

"Okay, kids. We are going for dinner. You guys try this trick on your father. I bet he has forgotten it."

On the way to the restaurant, I recalled, "You know, during that day, another funny thing happened."

"What was that?"

"I will tell you after our meals."

The restaurant served only vegetarian meals. While we waited for our order, I discovered that Vampira also liked seafood.

"Would you like to hear a joke I wrote about seafood?"

"Sure."

> A man went to a restaurant and ordered lobster. When the plate was placed before him, the lobster was in numerous pieces. The man asked the waiter, "Why is my lobster so broken up?" The waiter answered, "The creatures fight inside the tank and they break off each other's limbs." The man then said, "Okay, bring me the winner."

"I think I've read that somewhere."

"It was in Reader's Digest many years ago."

"Then, it is not a new joke."

“I improved it.”

“How?”

The waiter agreed with the customer, went to the kitchen and came back after a few minutes. When the new plate was placed before him, the man noticed that the new lobster was mostly intact but it had two parts detached. He said, "This one does not have a claw and something else too." The waiter said "Sir, this is indeed the victor but victory cost him an arm and a leg."

“Okay. That was funny.”

“How about another?”

“You seem to be on a roll and I don’t think I can stop you now.”

“Are you familiar with blonde jokes?”

“No. Jokes about blondes?”

“Well, if you are not familiar with them then it may not be as funny as it is meant to be.”

“So, what? I will give it a try.”

“Well, these jokes assume that blondes are very dumb.”

“Oh, you mean dumb-blonde jokes? I may have come across them somewhere but I cannot recall any.”

“Well, this joke is not necessarily a dumb-blonde joke but it is about East Asians… Chinese or Japanese who often replace their Rs with Ls and vice versa.”

“Proceed.”

A blonde goes to a Japanese restaurant. The blonde orders, “I would like a fried duck.” The waiter repeats the order as he writes it down on his notebook, “One duck fly.” The blonde ponders over this response and then says, “In that case, a fried chicken.”

“Nothing?”

“I think that duck joke just died in the water.”

“It does not matter. In the US, blonde jokes have become ‘politically incorrect’.”

“Because?”

“Ideally, blondes should not be offended because hair colour has no correlation to intelligence. Blondes look prettier than others. And, pretty people are often assumed to be intelligent as well. When the expectations do not match with reality, it gives rise to the opposite assumption that blondes must be stupid. It seems everyone's stupid."

"When jokes create the wrong impression about people, they should be banned."

"You cannot go around and start banning stuff left and right."

"If something is misused, then it should be banned. Like guns in America."

"Ban guns? ... Then, why don't we ban phones as well? A lot of gangsters use phones to make threat calls!"

"I don't know. Why do they need so many guns?"

"They have a gun culture. We don't. It is not for us to judge. We have a small but thriving stabbing and beheading culture. What would happen if knives were banned?"

She shook her head. "Maybe my example was bad but jokes that ridicule women should not be given respectability."

"What if men banned jokes that women make to make men look stupid?"

"No, those jokes are just funny."

"See? What is funny to you can be offensive to others. If we start banning things that someone considers offensive, then eventually everything will be banned. Only a tyrannical society will ban humour."

"When did blonde jokes stop being funny?"

"When they degenerated from being about intelligence to being just crass or double-meaning."

"Then, they are right to ban them."

"And destroy an entire class of great jokes created over decades? Anyway, my blonde jokes are clean, like all my jokes. The blondes are just a prop to say something funny or clever. In fact, in some of my blonde jokes, they are smarter than others."

"How?"

"In one blonde joke, a teacher asks a class if they can draw a square with three lines."

"And, the blonde drew a square with three lines?"

"She drew a square with less than three lines."

"Less than three lines? How?"

I took a paper towel, placed it flat on the table and drew a rectangle on it.

"That is a rectangle. Not a square. It has four lines."

I drew a line in the middle of the rectangle connecting the two broader sides.

"Now, you have two squares made from 5 lines. That is 2.5 lines per square."

"I can draw a square with two lines."

"How?"

She took the pen and the paper towel, and drew two lines like an L in the top-right corner. The two sides of the corner made the space enclosed by the two lines into a *de facto* square. I took the paper towel back and looked at her with admiration. "Man, you are smarter than I am! I'm going to to add this to my jokebook."

"No, it is my copyright."

"I will give your idea to a redhead. A brunette, a blonde and a red-head walk into a bar. They do not have money to pay for their drinks so the barman offers them a challenge first."

"I will give your idea to a redhead. A brunette, a blonde and a red-head walk into a bar. They do not have money to pay for their drinks so the barman offers them a challenge first."

"What are redheads? People with red hair? Does they even exist?"

"There are people with dark reddish-brown hair. They are called redheads. I do not think the bright red variety exists. I've not seen any. Female redheads are supposed to be hotter than the blondes and even more stupid."

"This is getting even more stupid than I thought it would be."

"There is another category of stupid."

"Is there?"

"Platinum blondes. Platinum blondes are even more stupid than... I don't know if they are more stupid than redheads but they are definitely stupider than blondes. Platinum does not have much yellow and is a lot more pale."

Vampira slowly shook her head and took the paper towel from me again. She said, "I shouldn't be doing this to my own kind." She then folded the corner of the square on the paper and then folded the paper diagonally. It now looked like an arrow. She then drew a line on one side of the folded corner and then continued it on the other side of the arrow tip. "There! One line. Give it to the platinum blonde."

Even before the prayer session, our class was in chaos and there was great excitement everywhere because all classes were cancelled that day. I found one group where one kid was excitedly telling a story. When he finished, a second kid seemed to become disappointed while everyone else laughed at him. I joined in and asked what was the story.

"Well, I was travelling in a bus recently and I asked a woman to get me a ticket. She haughtily refused to pass the money and get the ticket. Furious, I stole a big parcel she was carrying."

The idiot that I was had to ask, "What was in the parcel?"

"Your ass!"

"Yes. Only an ass will think it is possible for someone like to me steal a big parcel from a bus full of people."

I felt like a real idiot and I did the only decent thing any other kid in my place would have done. I got another kid to suffer the same fate. Even after that, I was not satisfied. I went around got another would-be victim. This second kid was a silent bully. He never went out of his way to bully anyone but because of his height and strength he could punish anyone who annoyed him. Added to that, there was already some bad blood between the teller of the tale and the bully. Game set. Match. Go!

When the kid finished his tale, the bully just smiled. He did not ask what was in the parcel. He probably thought there was more to the story. So, the kid says, 'Why don't ask me what was in the parcel?' The bully obliges, 'What was in the parcel?' 'Your ass,' came the reply. The bully's smiling demeanour vanished. 'My ass was in the parcel,' he asked. Then, he hit him. 'How dare you take my ass?' He grabbed at his belt. 'I want to take back my ass! Give my ass back!' He pushed him down and kicked his ass several times. I don't think that kid ever tried that story on anyone else after that.

"When you are young, you think your life is very boring. Looking back, now, it seems as if it was not so boring after all."

"My life was definitely boring."

"Even with the tattoos and the fangs?"

"Those are more recent. My school life was very unexciting."

I remained silent.

"There was one incident… that I think was out of the ordinary. We scared the heck out of some people. It is not a big deal really but back then..."

"What did you do?"

"Well, one weekend, two girls from my section and two girls from the other section of our class volunteered to help with an event that took place in our school. It was a national seminar or conference for teachers. It was a two-day event and we had to stay back in school on a Friday and a Saturday."

"They made girl students to spend the night at the school?"

"Ours is an all-girls school. The teachers were all women."

"All right."

"In the evening at around 7 o' clock, we had dinner. After that, the teachers left us. There was nobody to mind us. We roamed the dark and empty classrooms, taking care to avoid the block where our teachers and the attendees were housed. We had time on our hands but had nothing to do. Finally, we decided to call it a day and go to bed. Unfortuately, there were no beds. We had to sleep on the benches. Only one girl had the forethought to bring her own blanket. Everyone else thought the school will be providing us with everything. It was summer so this was not a real problem. Before we went to bed, we decided to go to the toilet. This place was at a far corner of the school compound. It was very close to the main road. In those days, our school was in an isolated stretch of the road. Our school bought that land outside of town because it was cheap. There were no houses on the other side of the road. It was empty for several kilometres. The only building nearby was a hospital, which also bought land outside of town because it was cheap. Between the hospital and our school, there was a bend in the road that was known as the 'Death Point'. The stretch of road near *Death Point* was mostly free of traffic and vehicles tended to speed up on it. A lot of accidents happened near Death Point and several lives were lost every year. The place was known to be haunted at night. With no street lights, Death Point spooked everyone. After passing Death Point, you have to go past our school."

She mapped the route with her hands and I nodded.

"The only built-up part of our school compound near the road was the students' toilet."

"... to aid the removal of sewage from the septic tank."

"Maybe. It was a full moon that day… In fact, it was the biggest moon I had ever seen. It was double the usual full moon size. I brought it to the attention of my friends but they did not find it unusual or exciting. They just looked at it and moved on to other things. It had zero impact on them. Anyway, we climbed on top of the toilet. I asked the tallest girl in our group to wrap the white blanket around her from head to toe. I asked her to stand in full view of the oncoming traffic while we hid on the steps. I asked her to beckon to oncoming two-wheeler riders to come closer. As the men approached, I asked the other girls let out blood-curdling screams. I remained on the ground to spot our victims. The tall girl's performance terrified everyone who passed us that night. The first guy was on a scooter."

"What happened?"

"He was travelling at a normal slow speed but when he spotted our ghost I saw him shift the gears up and scooted the hell out of there."

"Really?"

"The next guy was on a cycle. He saw us and he started pedalling furiously. He also left the area in a hurry."

"All the two-wheelers that we targeted like this behaved in the exact manner. All guys we harassed that night were cowards. Finally, one cycle guy stopped. He called out asking who it was. He seemed pretty sure that our ghost was a guy."

"He was not scared?"

"Listen to me. He stopped quite a distance from us and was afraid to pass. So, he tried to ask questions."

"What did you do then?"

"Well, I asked the rest of the girls cover their bodies with their dupattas and accompany our lead ghost. They got behind her and made quite a racket. The man started running on foot while he pushed his cycle on his side. He didn't even get on the seat. After he disappeared fro view, we climbed down and went back to our classroom."

"It must have been very exciting."

"It certainly was to us. I got my friends to promise not to tell anyone about our prank. I do not know if they kept it a secret. My guess is that anybody who heard the story would have thought we were just making it up."

After a few moments, I said, "So, you were an *enfant terrible* when you were young?"

"No. Only that day. I was overcome by some short-lived motivation to cause mischief and everything just clicked into place."

"I can't imagine you as a troublemaker."

"Looks can be deceptive, my friend," she said as she threw her hair backwards. "I had a friend who looked like a real angel. Nobody would suspect her of any mischief but she was a troublemaker like no other."

"For example…"

"Well, one day, I was with her in some science lab, physics or chemistry or biology, I don't know. There was nobody else there at that time. I was working on my observation notebook while she was meddling with a switchboard. Suddenly, she turns to me and says, 'You want to see something funny?' I say, 'What?'. She points to the switchboard and says, 'Press this switch.' I pressed it and the plug point exploded with fire and sparks coming out of it. All the lights went out. I grabbed my book and decided to run back to our class but my friend didn't seem to want to come with me. She just stood there as if nothing happened. 'Come on before we get caught,' I urged her. She just walked slowly behind me with her usual angelic face while I ran out of there like a frightened cat."

I didn't say anything.

"In the evening, we were in a games session when I noticed some stranger inspecting a large switching panel that we had in the auditorium. Some teachers were also with him and trying to help fix a problem. I didn't think much of it at that time but later that night I realized that the man must have been an electrician. He was called in to fix the damaged circuit in the lab."

"Your friend must have connected the live and neutral pins without a load when you pressed the switch. The short-circuit must have triggered a tripper. I do not think any damage was done. It must have been just a matter of identifying the tripper that was supplying power to the lab and turning it on again."

"My friend was least affected by it. Several times after that incident, when we were at the lab, she would point to a switchboard and ask, 'Do you want to try it again?'"

I laughed and said, "What is she doing now?"

"She is a physics teacher."

When we returned to the tree spot, the Sun had set and a full moon lit up the beach like a street lamp. If there was anything wrong with Vampira, I would know tonight.

The kids were back with their mother because there was no TV in the cottage.

"Tell us a scary story"

"Have you heard of *Naranathu Brandhan*?"

No, they had not.

"Well, he was a mad man who live long ago in Palakkad. He had elephantiasis in one leg and because of that he was not useful in any occupation. People believed that he was some sort of *yogi* and they fed him for free. Almost every day, he would roll up a huge rock to the top of a small hill. Once there, he would push the rock down the hill. Don't worry. The rock did not hit any houses because nobody lived around it. People thought he did this to demonstrate the futility of our normal human existence. We strive hard all our life accumulate wealth but in the end when we die we have to give up everything. One day or rather night... it was a full moon day like today, Naranathu Brandhan decided to sleep inside a graveyard. He was not afraid of ghosts or zombies or anything. But, the ghosts in the graveyard were very upset that a man had invaded their place and had shown no fear whatsoever. So, they started howling, screaming, shouting... creating all kinds of noise and racket to frighten Naranathu Brandhan and make him leave. Naranathu Brandhan was not frightened in the least. Instead, he thought they were funny and laughed at their antics. Throughout the night, they tried to frighten him but he failed to move. Towards dawn, they realized he was no ordinary human. Still, to compensate for their wounded pride, they offered him a wish. He could ask anything he wanted. He asked them if they knew how long he would live. They said they knew this and gave him the exact day, hour and minute that he was going to die. Then, he asked them, as his wish, that he live one more day extra. This, the ghosts said, they could not do as the date and time has already been set. So, he asked them if they could reduce his lifetime by one day. This also they refused as it would cause a mistake in their calculation of his lifetime. So, Brandhan said he did not want anything else. 'You have to ask something from us,' they insisted. 'All right,' he said, 'can you change this elephantiasis infection from this leg to the this leg'. The ghosts were surprised by his decision but because he was a *brandhan*, they accepted it. They magically transferred the swelling in one leg to his other leg. Then, the ghosts disappeared without troubling him further. That's the end of the story."

"It's not scary at all."

"It is a moral story. I did not write it. It is part of Kerala's folklore. However, I have written a scary exorcism story set in the USA. Would you like to listen to it?"

"What is an exorci..."

"When a ghost or evil spirit gains control over the mind and body of a person, it is known as demonic possession. The Christian Church has a way of driving out the ghost. The procedure is known as an exorcism. The concept became famous after a movie titled *The Exorcist* was released in the 70s. It is not really a scary movie but for the time it was and became a worldwide hit. Since then, several exorcism-based movies, TV programmes and books have been released."

"Why is it in the USA?"

"All exorcism movies are made in the US. I saw some of these movies and they were all in the US. My story is based on a nightmare I had after watching these movies."

"Okay. Tell us your story."

The Exorcist

"Do you know this place?" I asked the postman.

"This is where Mademoiselle Zuma lives."

"She is competition. You were supposed to tell me about these things."

"Was I?"

"Here is a twenty. If a new business like this opens, you tell me."

The money disappeared in a flash. "All righty then."

I knocked on the door. After quite a while, Zuma opened it. She tried to smile and gave up.

"You are that Indian guy."

"Right. This is my territory. I want you to leave."

"This is not India. You foreigners don't tell us anything."

"All right. I gave you a warning." I began to leave.

"You don't scare me," she shouted after me.

Business has almost dried up. The Indians here don't seem to be building anything. They are just buying up existing properties. What's left is palm-reading and horoscopes. Horoscopes is just computer software. I have the aptitude but not the attitude to do palm-reading. To make things worse, I have new competition. Zuma has a crystal ball, magic tricks and an outfit to match. I cannot compete with that. I don't wear traditional clothes. Putting on a show is not my thing. This world is for crooked crooks. It has no place for ethically honest crooks like me.

The future looked bleak when I got a call from someone who knew someone I knew. It was a case of demonic possession. A rich man had bought a Colonial mansion in the country where he planned to settle permanently. A few days after his family moved in, they heard some noises at night. During one of these episodes, they decided to check the room where their kid was sleeping and lo behold he was floating above the bed and speaking in a strange language with the voice of an old woman. The family tried to get help from the Church but they could not do anything. These episodes lasted only a few minutes and the boy was fine in the morning. However, he becoming less lively each day. The man, his wife and the kid came to see me.

"I don't do demonic possessions and I have no experience in it."

"We asked the Church and they couldn't do anything either. Not even Jesus Christ could help us."

"It is not that Jesus Christ cannot fix it. It is your faith in Him that is lacking."

"Is there something in Indian magic that you could try?"

"Indian magic? There is no such thing… maybe… I don't… Well, in the state of Kerala, there is a temple where ghosts used to be exorcised. The priest whipped the possessed person with a flexible stick… It is called a *pulliwaaral*. It is a green stick made from a tamarind tree branch. It is very strong and flexible. After about an hour or so of beatings, the ghost would not be able to endure the pain and leave the body. The possessed person had to be an adult to survive the ordeal. The practice is of course banned now. It was popular a long time ago… in the bad old days. The government is very strict about these things now."

"When was the last time such a procedure was carried out?"

"2006 or 2007. You see this stick? I can do the same exorcism if I wanted to. Doesn't require any talent. I just don't want to. So, let's try some peaceful methods to make this ghost leave."

"What do you suggest?"

"First, make your new home hostile to demonic spirits. Get rid of any larger-than-life statues, paintings or structures of animals, humans or mythical creatures. Remove all gargoyles and gnomes, for example. Humans should dominate the dwelling. Evil spirits should not think of it as a friendly place."

"It can be done."

"Place a photo or idol of your god in every room and near every bed. Any other photos or paintings should be about happy or positive things. No depictions of suffering, conflict, sex scenes, horned animals, and such. Get rid of all portraits, mirrors, beds or other personal-use items left by the previous owners. Burn them if they are not valuable. Ideally, you should be building a new house and using new furniture. For now, it is enough if you buy new articles for personal-use items."

"Anything else?"

"Most importantly, get an interior designer to repurpose the rooms in the mansion as per *Vastu Shastra*. Vastu Shastra is a traditional Indian treatise on building architecture. It is also known as the Indian *Feng Shui*. I will give you a book that I have written on the subject. Although Vastu Shastra is a based on a Hindu myth, it is actually a collection of time-tested house-planning best-practices. Its prescriptions are secular enough to be practiced like *yoga*. Under these circumstances, we should try everything."

"Will that help?"

"We have to see how strong the demon is and we can move on to more drastic measures if needed. And, do not leave this kid alone at night. There should be some adult in his room to protect him. He should not be left to fend for himself. Put a big portrait of your god in his room so that he feels safe. Get rid of any dolls in his possession. He is too old to play with them. Get rid of all posters and decorations in his room. Hey, kid, come here."

The kid left his bunny doll on his chair and walked towards me.

"Are you aware of this demon that's bothering you?"

"Yes!"

"Have you told it to stop bothering you?"

"No."

"Why not?"

No answer.

"Do you believe in Jesus Christ?"

He nodded.

"Who is he?"

"God."

"What is God?"

"The most powerful man in the Universe."

"Have you prayed to Jesus Christ to get rid of the demon?"

"Hmm…"

"You better! You see this stick?"

I hit my desk with it. The boy closed his eyes and slowly opened them.

"You pray to God to get rid of that demon. Do you understand?"

The boy nodded.

"Or else, I will skin you alive."

I pointed the stick at his chair and motioned him to go.

I addressed his parents.

"Don't lose hope. Follow the advice that I gave you earlier. We will fix this somehow. You make your kid memorize some prayers from the Christian prayer book. It will give him confidence. Make the person who stays in the room to recite the prayers with him if there are any disturbances."

"How much do we have to pay you?"

"For now, just pay for that book. You can give me a few hundred dollars if what I have prescribed does the job. If I have to come to your place, you will have to pay for all expenses." The expenses will always be more than the consultation. That's how this business survives.

They bought a copy of my book and left.

After a month, I received a call from the family. The levitations and weird voices had stopped. There were still weird noises and rattling on the windows. The boy suffered from nightmares and sleeplessness. Healthwise, he was not getting better.

Some years ago, I saw a Soviet movie called *Viy*. It was an unusual movie because it was a religious horror movie made under an atheistic censorship-loving regime. The story was about a monk defeating a witch and getting killed in the end. I was not willing to get killed but I was not going to give up without trying something.

The current situation required a personal visit. Hello, expenses! First, I bought an imported vintage *Jai Maha Kali Mantra* CD. Cost $100. I bought a Bluetooth portable speaker and USB pen drive. Cost... another $20. I ripped the CD to MP3 files. I copied the MP3 files to the USB drive. I played the USB drive on the speaker and the output was very good. I bought a giant scary Kali poster. Price... $20... I am being generous here. A packet of holy ash, also imported from India. $10. I received a paid-for first-class plane ticket but I exchanged it with a guy in coach who could not get one. The kid's family picked me up at the airport.

At their home, I told the parents that we will have to draw the demon out to reveal itself. We removed all the photos of Jesus Christ and other sacred articles from the kid's room. That night, the parents of the kid and myself staked out around the kid's bed. Around midnight, a chill breeze disturbed the room. A puma-like creature jumped in through the window. It then transformed into a 9- to 10-feet female demon. It had a thin body, long legs, burning eyes and fiery expression. It seemed to have no clothes but in the dark there was not much to see either. The demon approached the bed where the kid was sleeping. Soon, the kid was levitating above his bed.

I picked up the portable media player and turned it on. The sounds of *Maha Kali Mantra* filled out the room. For a small device, the output was phenomenal. The demon fell down. The kid fell back on the bed. The puma-like creature seen earlier materialized on the windowsill and jumped out.

The kid was still sleeping and we approached the bed. His father closed the window. We woke the boy up. He seemed all right and remembered nothing. We brought back the photos of Jesus Christ and other sacred articles into the room.

"What do you think we should do now?"

"I will have to speak to a higher power. I need a quite room."

The room was arranged. I went in and sat down in *padmasana*. I closed my eyes and meditated.

"I think the username is SwamiManikandeswara2001." I wrote it down on a piece of paper for them.

"The 'swomee' is available… even at this hour."

"It is daytime in India now. Where can he go? He is in jail."

"In jail?"

"He brainwashed the MD of our national stock exchange and tried to run it by proxy. Now, he is counting the bars in his cell."

"How can he be chatting on the Internet when he is in jail?"

"India is one of the freest countries in the world… if you have money. Everything will be available if you have money."

The swami came online. "Subhash, how are you? Long time no see. I wish you were here."

"That's why I left the country."

"You are a funny guy. Always joking. You should write a jokebook."

"Listen! I need your help."

"My help? Anything for my favourite disciple. Just ask me."

"Don't say that. The cops are listening. They will come after me."

"Okay. Say what you want."

"I'm working on a case involving the demonic possession of a kid. The demon is shaped like an animal."

"It is not a ghost?"

"No, not a ghost. It is not a dead person's ghost."

"Did you play *Hanuman Chalisa* or *Ma Kali Mantra*?"

"Yes, but the kid cannot chant Hindu mantras or recite Christian prayers all the time. The demon has to be permanently driven away."

"If it is an animal spirit, then it is very difficult. You will have to try black magic."

"That is very dangerous for everyone who gets involved. I don't know anyone who knows it. I don't want to know anyone who knows it."

"Look, Subhash. Why don't you give up these *tukda* operations and join the big league with me?"

"With you? You are in Tihar Jail!"

"So, what? All big VIPs of our great nation are here or have been here. Prime ministers, ministers, MPs, bureaucrats ..."

"... swamis like you ..."

"It is a rite of passage ..."

"I knew I shouldn't have called you."

I asked them to exit the chat. A crook finds that he has some unnatural power. He tries to exploit it for making money. He goes to jail. There, he makes contacts with politicians and government officials. Then, he becomes even more powerful! It is a strange world. Everyone's rolling in money except me.

"What do we do now?"

"I don't know. Let us get some rest now. I will think of something tomorrow."

Next day, I had breakfast with the family. I drove to town and made some purchases. I bought some rope. I asked for some drawing board chalk. I got the dust-free type. I wondered if the dust-causing chalk would make a difference. At a junkyard, I picked up a bottle of Absolut vodka and a piece of wine-bottle cork.

Back at the mansion, I removed all Christian idols and images like I did during the previous night. I hung the Kali poster on a line over the kid's bed. I rolled up the poster so that Kali remained hidden. I added some weights to the lower edge of the poster so that it could be unrolled when required. I got a music system installed and placed my CD in it. I tested it and the sound output was good.

During that night, we let the mother and kid sleep on the bed. The father and myself sat on the floor and played *snake and ladders.* I had my stick on my back behind my shirt. The father had the remote for the CD system and I had the portable speaker. The window was open and the demon could swoop in any moment if it wished to. If ever there was a welcome party for a demon, this was it.

Around midnight, a chill breeze filled the room. Our hair stood up. The doors rattled. I motioned to the father to take the chalk. He drew a circle around the bed. His wife drew crosses inside it. We then huddled on the bed. The puma-like creature jumped into the room and transformed into the female demon seen on the previous night.

"What are you going to do now?" the father asked me.

I tried to speak. No words came out. I tried again. Nothing.

The demon stood outside the circle and tried to lean and grab the kid. He and his mother backed up and fell down on the other side of the bed. I took my stick out and hit the demon's hand right in the middle. The demon grabbed me by the neck and slammed me back on the bed. The mother reached out to me.

"Say your prayers," I told her with difficulty.

I let the weights on the poster fall down. Maha Kali was in full view. The demon fell back. The father pressed the remote. The room was filled with the sounds of Kali mantra. I grabbed the holy ash and threw it on the demon on the ground. The demon became blind and started convulsing. By now, I was bold enough to step out of the circle. I threw the noose around its neck and tied the rest of the rope around its body. I then took my stick and proceeded to remove the hide off the demon's back. After probably around a 100 lashes, the demon was pretty much defeated. I threw more ash on it. It shrunk in size. I grabbed it by the leg and put it in the vodka bottle. I then corked the bottle tight.

I knocked on the door. Mademoiselle Zuma opened it.

"Well, hello, pretty boy!"

Then, her expression changed.

"You came here to cast an evil spirit on me?"

She tried to slam the door. It did not budge. She tried again. No luck. She retreated inside the house. The door slammed. I heard her scream several times. I turned to leave. Now, nobody is going to compete with… I need to get a new name. In this country, it makes people think of fast-food.

UNLIKELY
STORIES
Alien
Encounter

A few weeks after trapping the demon, I received a phone call from the father of the kid. He said everything was fine with his family but that he was making the call on behalf of a friend of his. That guy's kid was in high school. Of late, the boy has been complaining of being abducted repeatedly by an alien. He was terrified of living in his family home and instead wanted to go and live with his grandma in Florida. We arranged a meeting with the kid's father. The man was asked not to tell anyone, particularly his family members, about the meeting.

Like last time, a first-class plane ticket was arranged and I travelled in economy. I met the high-school kid's father in familiar surroundings.

"What kind of kid is he?"

"Well, he is average in studies. Outstanding in sports. A normal kid all along except during the last few weeks."

"Was there anything unusual that happened before that time?"

"Nothing. Except, me and my wife went on a European tour. When we came back after a month, he started telling these tales of being kidnapped by aliens and being subjected to unusual experiments."

"Proctology experiments?"

"Yes. And, lots of unexplained time loss."

"Was he interested in aliens and UFOs before your tour?"

"No."

"Then…"

"However…"

"Yes?"

"He never said anything about UFOs."

"Budget cuts, probably."

"I didn't get you."

"All UFO sightings and alien encounters are staged by the government."

"If the government is involved, can you help us?"

"I cannot. But, let us confirm that that is the case first."

"Where is your kid usually when these aliens show up and probe him?"

"At our home. He says he shouts like hell but nobody comes to help him."

"You never hear anything?"

"Nothing. Neither does my wife. Even our dog does not raise an alarm."

"How often does this occur?"

"Every two or three days."

"What happens during these alien encounters? What kind of aliens are they?"

"He says they are two-legged human-like aliens with a large head and very large eyes and frog-like arms and feet."

"He does not fight them?" I threw soft punches in the air like a boxer. "You know, put up a fight?"

"No. He says that after a while his body becomes paralysed and is unable to shout any more. He remains conscious for a few more minutes before his eyes become shut. He remembers being carried out of the room in the arms of the alien and after a minute or so he blanks out. He does have snatches of memory... of being probed in the rear. It happens in a room with a lot of lights that are so bright he cannot open his eyes. The only time he can open his eyes is when the alien obstructs the lights with its large head. What he manages to see at that time is even more scary because the alien is always seen holding a very long instrument in its hand. When the boy finally wakes up, he is back in his bed."

"Have you tried to reassure him in any way?"

"Yes. For several days, we all... me, my wife and my kid... camped out in the living room. We also had our dog with us. He still says the same thing happened."

"Nothing unusual was recorded in your CCTV cameras?"

"Nothing."

"Okay. I will give you a device. It will have a wire. You wrap its free end around some large metallic object like a steel water pipe near the kid's room. After say nine or ten days, you remove the

Micro-SD card in it and mail it to me. Ensure that nobody follows you when you go to the post office."

Back at my hideout… my place, I built a low-power data logger using two ATtiny chips, an RTC module and a memory card module. It has an on-off switch and a battery pack that can last several months. The device did nothing more than record the time every minute in an encrypted text file on the SD card. I mailed it to the guy who requested the exorcism and asked him to personally and discretely hand over the device to his friend.

Two weeks later, I received the SD card at the post office. I examined the data log on my computer and found that the device had been reset four times during the time it was on. All of them at night at around two o' clock.

I then asked them to send me the CCTV hard disks. The footage had cuts around the same time the data logger had reset. The cuts lasted an hour or so. Otherwise, there was nothing unusual.

I did not tell the man I had come to visit him. I had rented a motorcycle and an aftermarket muffler. The compact vehicle was now quieter than usual. At the town, I stopped at a hardware store and bought a crowbar. I then rode towards the man's place. I parked the vehicle in a wooded area near his compound and covered it with a black cover. I had brought a drone with me and spent a few hours surveying his homestead. The house stood on a large plot of land with tall trees surrounding it in all directions. There was a garage next to the house. It was not locked. Inside, they had several cars, old and new, all polished and shiny. When darkness fell, I got my sleeping bag out. I set an alarm for a quarter to two and went to sleep.

When I woke up, it was much colder than I expected. I put on a mask. I checked my camera and put it in my pocket. I took out the crowbar and walked over to the man's compound. The moon was bright and I did not need a torch. I went through the fence and moved as quickly and silently as possible. I then took refuge in a tree that had good view of the house. Nothing happened the entire night. Or, the next night.

On the third day, I was riding the motorcycle from the town to my hideout when from a distance I spotted a van parked in the woods. I turned the motorcycle around and rode to the woods on the other side of the compound. I hid the motorcycle as best as I could and walked over to the side where the van was parked.

I used the zoom lens to take photographs of the van and its license plate. There were no glass windows so I did not know if anyone was in it. There was no way to check the front of the vehicle, as it was parked very close to some trees. Also, I did not want to alert the van occupants to my presence. I bet they were reconnoitring the area like I had so I returned to where my motorcycle was hidden. I got my sleeping bag out and set my alarm to a quarter past one.

I got up feeling miserable like in the previous nights. This gig is not worth the effort if I did not find an alien. I went to the woods on the other side and lo behold an alien stepped out of the van! It walked over to the fence and crossed into the compound in the same place that I had used in the previous two nights.

I quickly checked the van from a different vantage point to see if there was anyone else in it. The van was dark. I used the zoom lens on the windshield and I could notice no presence.

I crossed over the fence at another place and followed the alien to the house. A few minutes later, several lights in the house lit up simultaneously and went dark again. The main door opened and the alien walked out carrying an unconscious tall young man in its hands. In the moonlight, I noticed something else strange. The young man's father and I assume his wife were standing on the first floor. They were just standing motionless near the glass front looking over the alien who was taking their kid away.

I followed the alien back to the fence. The alien passed the kid across the fence with some difficulty. This was no alien! It must be a man.

The alien man picked up the boy again and walked towards the van. I did not know if the alien man had backup in the van so I decide to make contact then and there, far away from the van. I took the crowbar out, sprinted towards the alien and plunged the metal into the back of the alleged creature from outer space. The alien man and the kid fell down. I then distinctly heard a man crying in pain but it was not coming from the kid. He was still unconscious. I hit the alien man several times on the legs so as to immobilize him. The suit seemed to protect him. Then, I took several potshots to the head. After a dozen hits, the alien man became motionless. I took a few photographs and took cover behind some trees. I zoomed the lens on the van. No movement there.

I crept over to the van. I picked up a big rock and smashed it on the windshield. I took cover again. Nothing moving. I took my torch out and flashed it inside the van. The driver's cabin was empty. The sliding doors were locked. I put my ear to the sides of the van and I heard nothing. I let the air out of the tyres because I was very annoyed. I took several photographs of the van. I went back to the fence. The alien man had not moved. Neither had the boy. Emboldened, I tried to grab the hood of the alien man. After several hits with crow bar, it came off. I shined the torch on the alien man's face. He had a human face but only an alien mother could have liked it. The man was bleeding. The blood loss was not heavy so he will live. I took a few more photographs of the man and his damaged suit. I pulled the remainder of the suit from his body. There were lights inside the suit. It was still powered on. Some sort of clear fluid oozed out of the suit. It must be a coolant or a hydraulic liquid. The man was wearing close-fit sports clothing over his body. I took photographs of that. Then, I stripped him of that clothing too. He seemed human except maybe for his ugly face. More photographs. The man had showed signs of serious trauma to his legs but the bones were not broken.

I picked up the young man in my hands. He weighed a tonne. What kind of food do you have to cook for them to weigh like this? I carried him over the fence but after that I dragged him by the neck. After some distance, he showed signs of consciousness. I dropped him. The boy sat up and then stood up. He startled when I moved. I asked him not to be afraid. "The alien that was bothering you is not really an alien." I took my camera out and showed him the photos on its display. "Let's go and see your parents. They are in some sort of trance." His parents were still standing motionless when we reached the house. "Listen. I will give you some instructions. Approach your parents without making a sound. Grab them gently from behind and get them to to lie down on the floor. Sprinkle or splash some water on their faces until they wake up. I think they will be fine. You will need to call an ambulance for that alien guy. Don't worry about the police. When they see the alien suit, they will stop asking questions. If they put too much pressure on you or detain you, ask them to talk to the military. Don't volunteer much information about me. You understand everything? Now, go." I watched from outside the house and the kid did what he was told. The parents seemed to recover quickly and I went back to where my motorcycle was hidden.

"Two suits are outside. One is at door. The other is in a car."

I checked who it was. A man in a suit wearing dark shades. Pigs are the worst human beings in the world!

"My days as an illegal immigrant are over. I've completed all paperwork."

"I'm not from Immigration. I'm from the FBI."

He showed me his badge.

"This? I have one just like that. It is nice to meet some fellow scammers but I'm expecting some customers today. So, go away and don't come back."

"Wait, I just want to talk. I want to confirm a few things. I will not bother you again."

I gestured to the douchebag to come in.

"If you are selling something, I'm not buying. I have no money."

The douchebag sat down.

"One year ago, you attacked a man in a van very grievously. He was a contractor for the Department of Defense. You also took a lot of photographs. We would like to have those photographs and all copies. We will not charge you with breaching national security if you cooperate. We have secret courts to punish offenders. We are being lenient because you have not tried to go public with the information you have."

I took a USB drive from my desk and gave it to him. "I knew you weren't the FBI. Anyway, you got what you wanted. Now, get lost."

The douchebag stood up and took out a wand-like device from his coat.

"Now, if you look here..."

"Don't look!" Zuma shouted as she rushed in. "He is trying to erase your memory,"

I avoided the flash and punched the guy in the guts. He bent forward and dropped the gadget. I kicked him on the chin and he fell back. He was motionless. I stepped on his fingers and he was still out cold. I took the USB drive from his coat. I then picked up the wand from the floor. It had some mighty heft to it. On further examination, I found that it had a slide switch. I did not turn it on. You could have easily mistaken the thing for some fancy fountain pen.

I knocked on the window and gestured to the man to get out.

"Hey, what's happening?"

The pig stepped out of the car and walked over to his colleague whom I had left leaning on the back wheel.

"He is hurt. What did you do to him?"

"He fainted and hurt himself."

He grabbed a wireless set from his belt. I kicked him in the ass and he collapsed on the other guy. He clumsily tried to get up. I kicked him on the chin. His head hit the other guy's head and the other guy woke up. Now, both were holding their heads in their hands. I took the wand out and switched it on.

"Guys… fellers… look here. You were never here. You do not work for the government. There was no investigation. Just go back to your parents' home and stay there."

The wand turned off automatically. The pigs passed out. I waited for them to wake up. After a while, I poured some water on their faces. I then had to help them both to get into the car. After a few minutes of fumbling, they drove off.

<hr>

"What are you going to do with the wand?""

"Can I use it on you?"

"No."

I wondered what to do with it.

"What are you doing to do with it?"

"I don't know. If someone else comes for it, we can use it on them."

"How many people did they hit with this thing? The EMTs. Hospital staff. Police. The kid and his parents."

"I wonder if the news got to the Press. Imagine how many people they would brain-block if it went to the Press."

"Journalists couldn't spot an alien if it walked right past them."

"These suits didn't do any better. It took them more than a year to find me."

"You are bitter because you couldn't make any money from that gig."

"A net loss. Three nights out in the biting cold for nothing."

"It's better than jail. You should count your blessings."

I put the tablet down. "What do you think?"

"Well… Inadequate world building. Inadequate character development. More tell than show."

"With all that, you will be in a coma. This is a narration, not a film flashback."

"How come Zuma is living with the narrator? Didn't he try to kill her?"

"Love does not follow logic. She liked what she saw. He is an Indian crook who escapes to the West. Zuma is a member of the Romani community, who are descendants of an Indian tribe that got lost in Europe hundreds of years ago. The Roma are often associated with petty crimes and have been persecuted for it. Zuma must have felt he could be reformed and put to good use in her business. How she survived is in another story."

"She has a roundabout way to hook up with someone of her own kind. Somebody should introduce her to a matrimony website or dating app."

"Some people… even in this day and age may be crazy enough to be romantic. After all, everything a person puts in their online profile must be true. If a girl says she is healthy, it does not mean that she is fat. If she says she is fat, it does not mean that she checks her weight every morning on a Richter scale."

"All right! And, it seems that you don't believe in aliens."

"No."

"So, you are saying, in the 5 billion years of its existence, Earth was NEVER visited by aliens?"

"According to a THEORY, the Universe began from nothing some 15 billion years ago. Only scientists can come up with that kind of nonsense. Everything out of nothing. Somewhere between that time and now, Earth along with other galaxies and solar systems and planets started developing as the Universe expanded. Earth did not exist on Day One."

"So?"

"Living beings on other planets with life had as much chance of visiting other planets with life as we did on Earth. If we did not find alien planets with life, it is quite likely that other planets with life did not either. The Universe has expanded so much for so long that the planets with life would have been separated by too much distance by now. Mathematically, the odds of two planets with life-supporting systems being within reachable distance is almost zero.”

“Almost?”

“There is a rare possibility that several planets in a solar system experience similar conditions and develop life. These life forms may have progressed to accomplishing inter-planetary travel. Forget about interstellar or intergalactic travel. Unfortunately, Earth is not among them. No other planet in our solar system has the same conditions as us.”

“I still think aliens must have visited us.”

“What happened when Europeans landed in the Americas? Or, in our own country?”

“The natives got the Bible and the visitors got the land.”

“Jomo Kenyatta.”

“Desmond Tutu.”

“Well, the invaders looted and killed wherever they went. If there is an alien civilization nearby that can conquer the distances required for inter-stellar travel, then it would have already made its appearance and destroyed us.” I paused. “To support such technological advances, their planet would have had a lot of resources… much better than ours. Then again, if they had all those resources, why would they come to Earth? Even if they did, they would have to travel at very high speeds. If they even crash into a speck of interstellar material, their spacecraft would have pulverized to dust.”

“Then, how do you explain all those monuments… in Egypt and other places… built thousands years ago with giant cuts of perfectly shaped monolithic rocks. They had alien technology.”

“Why should it be alien technology? Why couldn’t it be that ancient humans were capable enough to accomplish those feats?” Silence. “You see, in our history books, they say that between 4000 BC and 2000 BC, it was the Stone Age. So, according to historians, every human settlement around the world was strictly practising Stone Age customs and fashions. But, on 1 January, 1999 BC, *Time* magazine issued a special edition saying ‘Welcome to the *Bronze*

Age!'. On reading that, humans all over the world threw away their stone implements and switched to metallic power tools. That happened? Stone Age and Bronze Age are fancy names created by historians in Europe. They just expanded their limited world view of the European civilization to the rest of humanity. There were lots of non-European civilizations that were much more advanced than Europeans. Gold was used by Egyptians five thousand years ago. Just imagine how long it would have taken Egyptians to progress from being a bunch of hunter-gatherers to start mining, refining, minting, trading, selling and possessing gold. The Egyptians were refining gold when the Flintstones of Europe were still moving around in feet-powered cars. The Stone Age or Bronze Age timelines cannot be used in Egypt, India or China. The history books in our country just blindly accept whatever the Europeans say is history."

"So, there were ancient civilizations far ahead of our age?"

"Definitely."

"And, the men who lived at that time had technology to cut huge monolithic rocks and build monuments like the pyramids?"

"Have you heard about Stephen Hawking?"

"The physicist?"

"Yeah."

"What about him?"

"Stephen Hawking was you know a quadriplegic. He communicated his thoughts using just one cheek muscle and a human-computer interface. He allegedly wrote entire books with it."

"Everyone knows that."

"Do you know about his personal life?"

"Like what?"

"He was married and had several kids before he became afflicted. He had to be looked after by three nurses. Even in that condition, he was not only unfaithful to his wife but also deliberately inflicted mental cruelty on her. His wife left him. After some time, he divorced the nurse too. If a wheelchair-bound guy can do all that, why can't fully endowed humans put their brains together and accomplish superhuman feats like the pyramids?"

"So that's your take from the great scientist's life?"

"I don't think he was a great physicist. As a troublemaker, you have to admire his cheek."

"Please!" She shook her head. "You think you are better than scientists, don't you?"

"Shakespeare said all the world is a stage and everyone's an actor. I say the world is full of scams and almost every other person is a scamster. If you are not a scamster, you get fooled by a scamster. The world is full of crooks. Here, a crook! There, a crook!"

"Everywhere a…"

"Crook! Crook!"

"So Stephen Hawking is a crook?" She shook her head. "I don't believe it."

"We have been conditioned to blindly trust certain people and unquestioningly accept the narratives built around them. Most of the time, our brain does a good job of telling us what the scams are. But, we ignore it. We trust others who we think are smarter than us. Take, for example, the *Mona Lisa* painting by Leonardo Vinci. We have been told that she is the most beautiful woman ever or something hyperlative like that. What is your personal opinion of the painting? Do you have Internet on your phone? Do a search." I did not carry a mobile. My mobile is not a smartphone. It is an old-style Nokia feature phone. It does phone calls and SMS. That's it. Vampira took her phone out and did an image search for the painting. Do a search. Judging solely by your brain and not influenced by the urban legend that accompanies it, how does she look? Is she beautiful? Does she look human at all? Is she smiling? What is so enigmatic about her smile?"

"Well, it is strange that she does not have eyebrows. She looks like she has a gland problem or some developmental disease."

"But, you did believe…"

"She has eye bags. Her body is disproportionate. Maybe she was overweight. Her hair is short and thin. She may have had a serious hairfall problem."

"What do you…"

"She has multiple issues."

"You think…"

"It is an unremarkable painting of an unremarkable woman. Whoever said she was beautiful… It is a scam!"

"Right. We trust the hocus pocus. As Hitler said, a big lie is more believable than a small lie because vast majority of people tell small lies all the time. In the primitive simplicity of their minds, they think that it is not possible for someone to fabricate colossal untruths. Our overlords take advantage of this fact and exploit us. They know it is difficult to play with facts so they distort our reality by messing with our emotions and psychological weaknesses."

"You are now quoting Hitler?"

"Ah! That... That is another mistake that most people commit. If Hitler had said one plus one is two, will it become false? Bad people do not say wrong stuff all the time. What they do is say a lot of profound things and then sneak in a falsehood or an evil idea in it. That's what makes them dangerous."

"Con artists will always be there but that does not make you better than scientists."

"Why should I think a scientist is better than me? It is just a job. Not many of them are good at it. At best, they are one-trick ponies. Outside of their jobs, they are no different than an illiterate guy who pulls a rickshaw."

"And, you are better?"

"I'm the best in my line of business. You don't believe it? I will throw you a challenge. Hmm... What was special about the year 2000?"

"The new millennium? Y2K problem?"

"That year was not the beginning of the new millennium. The second millennium ended that year. The third millennium started in 2001. Everyone learns in school that there is no year zero. I knew that. Some other ordinary people also remembered it and complained. But, the scientists never complained. They joined everyone else celebrating the wrong year."

"Oh, that definitely makes you better!"

"I got lots more but... Anyway... What I really wanted say was..." I scratched my chin and thought hard. "The fundamental flaw in the approach of historians is that they rely entirely on evidence they can dig out and examine under a microscope."

"Can carbon-date."

"Right. If man lived in a house made of brick-and-mortar, it would last only a few decades. If instead he lived in a cave, then his belongings or doodles can survive millennia. Historians will believe a man who lived in a cave and refuse to accept the possibility that a man from a more advanced civilization could have simultaneously existed outside the cave in an ordinary house. Large parts of India has been continuously populated for thousands of years. But, Western historians say North Indians are descendants of Aryan shepherds who moved from Central Asia and settled in the Indus Valley. They believe in this premise because the ancient residents of the towns of Harappa and Mohenjadaro moved out for some unknown reason and nature had preserved the two towns for posterity. It is much more difficult to find ancient artefacts in say Connaught Place, New Delhi, because people have been living there forever."

"I give you that."

"Historians will every now and then change their timeline and give bizarre answers to fit the new data to their old theories. I read one news report where researchers found that native American communities had established themselves in the Andes mountains 12,800 years ago. This was two thousand years earlier than what historians thought was the case. You know what explanation the historians gave for this big hole in their timeline?"

She shrugged.

"It was a land rush, a free-for-all. The first inhabitants of South America RACED through the continent!"

"Like in the movie *Cannonball Race*?"

"Exactly. Even the story that man originated in Africa is bogus. Did dogs originate in Egypt? Did cats originate in China? Did cows originate in India? Everything had to originate from one location. Like in the Bible. It only helps the globalists promote the fallacy that we are all migrants and that our lands do not belong to us. And, that our land and its resources should be ceded to a world government run by unelected Fascists and plutocrats."

Vampira seemed to be thinking and after a while she said, "You know people in the West believe that all mankind originated from just two individuals — Adam and Eve. If that is true, then the human race was born out of siblings."

"No, you are making some wrong assumptions. The Bible says Eve was created from Adam and they had two kids — Cain and Abel. Cain kills Abel after a dispute over a barbecue and then their God condemns him and his future descendants. Cain leaves the Garden of Eden and moves to the Land of Nod. This land of Nod must have been already populated because Cain was able to find a dame there dumb enough to marry an axe-murderer. With her, Cain sired a line of prophets that ended in Jesus Christ. Where did Cain's wife come from? Like Eve, who was a pain in Adam's side, Cain's wife was created by God as were other dwellers in the land of Nod. So, there was no inter-marriage between siblings. There are other big holes in their belief system but this is not one of them. If one goes around looking for mistakes, you will find such things in every religion."

She nodded.

"That reminds me of Mark Twain who said that it was God's fault for banning the *apple of knowledge*, the forbidden fruit of the forbidden tree in the Garden of Eden. Twain wrote that if God had forbidden the snake, Adam would have eaten the snake and everything would have…"

Vampira started laughing but the kids interrupted.

"I don't understand anything."

"No more discussion. Read the next story."

"Just a second, honey," she told the kid and then turned to me, "What about the many UFO sightings? Not all of them are unreal."

"Well… One day, some years ago, around 3 o' clock in the afternoon, I saw a bright light shining and blinking in the sky. It was very big and I thought it might be a UFO. However, after a minute or so, the light stopped blinking and a tiny object that was shaped like a plane turned to the right and proceeded towards the horizon where the airport was located. What had really happened then was that the rays of the Sun were getting reflected on the sides of the plane and its windows made the reflection to blink. I had another experience, when I was a kid, involving a shining object in the sky. This was a very big pink object. It descended very rapidly. Hot pink gases escaped as it went below the tree line. At that time, I did not know what it was. I read a news report of a similar object observed near the Chennai airport. The personnel there spotted it but could not see where it landed. They also did not know what it was. Several years later, after our country had started importing firecrackers from China, these lights could be easily seen on Diwali nights. It was some kind of fireworks. Most UFO sightings are just regular aircraft, weather balloons or fireworks."

"I have seen videos of objects that look exactly like flying saucers that hover in the sky. They move faster than jet aircraft."

"If you have seen laser shows, then you will realize that these UFOs are images projected on the clouds, not real alien craft. Have you ever seen a video where the UFO hovers at tree-top level on a clear cloudless day? I bet 'never'."

"Are you saying that UFO sightings are just laser projections?"

"I think that it may be possible to build super-high-speed motors using superconductors and supercooled liquids. These motors cannot be used outside Earth's atmosphere. They cannot propel a craft in vacuum. Even on the inside, such motors will create highly destabilizing levels of turbulence, heat and sound. If a government can overcome those problems, they may be able to create UFO-like crafts. If the crafts moved at those speeds at low altitudes, there will be lots and lots of broken glass panes and other property damage. There will also be lots of injuries and deaths. The public will not like that."

"Why then do you think these governments act so hush-hush about UFOs? They must have something to hide."

"They want other countries to think they have alien technology and be afraid. They also don't want other countries to know how weak or strong their air defences are. In 2013, a giant fireball was noted in the sky in Russia. Its initial approach was not detected because it was obscured by the Sun. Now, if you want to nuke Russia or for that matter any other country, just follow the Sun and throw a giant rock."

"So, to mislead rival militaries, these countries put on UFO laser shows and stage alien encounters. That's what you believe?"

"Yeah. They kidnap their own citizens and probe them, hypnotise them and place false memories in their heads."

"And, there is no real alien technology? Area 51 is just a hoax?"

"If they had alien technology, it would have been already deployed in the battlefield. Area 51 belongs to US Department of Energy, not the Department of Defense. It is a site designated for nuclear decontamination. This has been revealed in several lawsuits filed by employees who had suffered radiation-related illnesses. Despite gag orders, the lawsuits have been reported in several newspapers. The US military sponsors a lot of TV programmes and movies, and they ask directors and producers to spread UFO or alien theories about the place."

"If you don't believe in aliens or UFOs, then you don't believe in time travel or the Theory of Relativity? Einstein must have been a fool... in your opinion."

"I don't know the actual physics about the Theory of Relativity. But remember that Einstein received his Nobel Prize for the photoelectric effect, not his blabberings about relativity."

"I guessed right you were going to deny it!"

"There are rumours that he relied so much on his first wife to solve his mathematical work that he split his prize money with her... after divorcing her."

"So, time-travel was her idea?"

"No, the idea belonged to several people throughout the ages. He is the one credited with associating science to it. The difficulty in accepting his claims stems from the fact that he did not have any qualifications to publish scientific theories. There are some rumours floating around since his own time that his predictions were actually made by other physicists and even his wife. Einstein worked at the patents office. It is not exactly a place for publishing theoretical physics but it does kindle your suspicion. If you look at his actual claims, almost everything is counter-intuitive. Light bends over matter, which everyone knows and has observed. In the absence of matter, light cannot bend... whatever be the gravitational force. I also don't believe that you can inflect time. It is an even more idiotic supposition. It is like looking at an old photo and believing you are still that young. You can take a clock, travel at any speed to anywhere in the universe and when you return, the clock would not have lost or gained a second when compared clocks that stayed on earth. If you look at a star that is say six light years away, you are looking at an image that was created six years ago. On that star, six years would have passed. The tiny light you see at great distances is not the real thing. The light that takes six years to reach Earth or 12 years at another interstellar location are just different images, not current events on the star. It is like the parallax illusion. It is your perspective that is becoming funny at different places and speeds, not time. Besides that, the same universe cannot experience in different times, then matter and energy will have to be duplicated. In my jokebook, I wrote a *Rajnikanth Fact,* on the lines of *Chuck Norris Fact...*

"What is that?"

"Chuck Norris is the American counterpart for Rajnikanth. Like Rajnikanth, he also does unbelievable stunts. On the Net, you will find a lot of Chuck Norris jokes, which are not supposed to be jokes

but actual facts. Some Indians have copied his *facts* and made
Rajnikanth Facts. Some Rajnikanth Facts are original and just as
funny."

"Such as…"

"… such as when Rajnikanth went to get a two-wheeler driving
license, he made the RTO chief do an 8. Or, when a meteorite tries to
hit him, it becomes classified as a meteor."

"Oh, okay."

"One Rajnikanth Fact that I wrote was that when Rajnikanth had
to write the answer for one divided by zero, he wrote the actual
answer instead of 'indeterminate'. Another one was that when you or
I try to subtract infinity from infinity, the answer is 'indeterminate'
but for Rajnikanth it is always zero. Even though we cannot possibly
know how big the universe is and assume it is infinite, matter and
energy making up the universe cannot exist in infinite time slices.
Time is the only constant. For scientist morons, it may not be. So, in
my humble opinion, Einstein is an elaborate hoax like Lincoln,
Mandela and Mother Teresa. Or, modern art."

"Lincoln, Mandela, Mother Teresa or modern art?"

"Mandela was trained as a Communist at an Israeli camp.
Communism was initially a wholly owned Jewish enterprise. Lenin
was sent to Russia in a train with gold supplied by a Wall Street bank.
Communism was brought to Russia by Jewish revolutionaries but it
was financed by Western capitalists. When the Communists captured
power in Russia, they imprisoned, killed and uprooted tens of
millions of Christians. They targeted some Jews too but most of their
victims were Christian. Their Utopian policies caused crop failures
and famine. In Ukraine, four million people died. Stalin was a
Georgian but to this day ethnic Ukrainians blame Russians. Stalin's
wife was Jewish. His government and secret police was mostly run by
Jewish Communists. They were also in charge of the labour camps.
Some of these Communists left for Israel. There, they did what they
knew best — create even more Soviet-style co-operatives. The *kibbutz*
is not an Israeli invention. It is a Soviet institution. The US had
Mandela on a terror list until 2008. The American government helped
South African authorities arrest Mandela, which resulted in his
incarceration for 27 years. He was a real terrorist though and his ANC
party was and is a violent organization. When Rajiv Gandhi started

raising a stink about apartheid and brought international sanctions against White-run South Africa, it became clear that the racist policies of that British colony would have to end once for all. So, how did they decide to retain the diamond mines while relinquishing power to the natives? They rehabilitate Mandela, finance a PR campaign, you know, complete with a concert in London and the rest is history. Mother Teresa also became an overnight celebrity after a PR campaign. A documentary was produced and she became world-famous. People started sending her outfit a lot of money. If there was an earthquake somewhere, the charity would receive donations. Her charity would just put the money in their bank account and do nothing about it. They weren't going to participate in any relief effort, at least not everywhere as people believed they would. Another fallout from Mother Teresa's deification is the persistent belief in the West that people in city of Calcutta are just dying in the streets and the *Missionaries of Charity* has an army of selfless Christian volunteers who went around and saved the helpless heathen from certain death. The name Calcutta became so badly associated with death and squalor that the milk-toast Communists who ruled West Bengal opted for the simpler alternative of changing the name of the city from Calcutta to Kolkatta. For a new generation of Westerners, *black hole of Calcutta* acquired a new meaning."

"There are lakhs of missionaries engaged in social service worldwide but they treat Mother Teresa as if she had done something no other missionary has done."

"When I first came to this city, I met an old blonde lady at the bus terminal. She was wearing a salwar-kameez, as if she were an Indian. She was also walking around in rubber slippers like a poor Indian. She said she was a missionary. She was lost like I was. There were no signs in English. Even the bus numbers were in the local script. I helped her order some tiffin at a stand-in restaurant. I asked her how she could be travelling all alone in a foreign country. She said, 'I am not alone. The Lord is with me.'"

Vampira just nodded.

"There are thousands of selfless people like that foreign lady. Fans of Mother Teresa seem to think she is the only one. When people ask how Christianity has spread all over the world but our belief system with its superior philosophy has remained confined to just this country, I say, 'Good marketing!'"

Vampira laughed. "No, we don't go around converting people. We respect their beliefs. Nobody becomes a Hindu. We are born Hindus."

"There are Hindus in Indonesia. The Ankor Wat temple in Kampuchea or Cambodia was a Hindu temple. It was the result of an Indian invasion. What really happened is not known. Was there coercion? Anyway, Buddhism, which started in India, has spread all over East Asia. It is in Thailand, Vietnam, Laos, Singapore, China and Japan. This was the result of peaceful but active conversion efforts. It is very un-Indian-like. Some people believe that the Hindu religion was the predominant religion in ancient times all over the world. There are historical records of Brahmins and temples in faraway locales such as Europe. I think it was just polytheism with some token presence of Hindu Brahmins who may have been shipped there for some reason. Hinduism is a civilization. Not a religion. Most of our culture is how our communities have evolved over time. It is deeply intertwined with religion but there is no book that says this is our culture."

"The Jews have a temple. Temple of Solomon or something."

"It was a temple with nothing in it. A Roman general sacked Jerusalem and destroyed the temple. He was curious and wanted to know what was in the room where the main deity or altar was located. This room was off-bounds for everyone except the high priests I think. When his soldiers bust into the room, there was nothing in it! It was an empty windowless room. The temple officials collected a lot of money from pilgrims... pilgrims not from Palestine... Hellenic Jews had settled all over the Roman empire. Like Muslims visiting Mecca today, Jews from all over the Mediterranean would go on a pilgrimage to Palestine and visit the temple. The temple collected money and gold for performing rituals in this room but the room by itself had nothing. That was because the Jews believed God had no form but they choose to keep the details secret."

"Wasn't the Ark stored there?"

"Not in that room but inside the temple. Not surprisingly, the Ark disappeared. The stories of Adam and Eve, the Great Flood, Abraham and others are not from Judaism. Jews claim they are but these stories have been part of the folklore of several non-Jewish people all over the Levant, that is, the Middle East, which is strangely in the Western part of Asia."

"It didn't come from the Old Testament?"

"No. The main books of the Old Testament are also part of the Jewish Bible. These were written in the first millennium in A.D, not B.C. The stories of the Creation and the prophets pre-existed in that area for thousands of years before Jews appropriated it. Jews learned about them during their Babylonian Captivity... when they were in Iraq. They were not very civilized until then. They were polytheistic and also practiced in devil worship and even indulged in human sacrifices. Later, they wrote books claiming they were being persecuted for their monotheistic beliefs. They were well-known practitioners of bizarre forms of torture but they claimed that it was the Babylonians who tortured them. They were in trouble because of their elites' involvement in brigandry and human trafficking. You see Palestine is on the crossroads between Europe, Asia and Africa. Invading armies had to pass through it. One army would sell their POWs to them and another army would retaliate because of that. So, Jews had to hunt with the hound and also run with the hare. Palestine was a godforsaken place where nothing grew so most of the population were a pastoral people. The elites, on the other hand, were essentially criminals... because I guess their guidance counsellor was not very good. Even today, I find that Jewish rabbis get involved in similar crimes. Some years ago, a journalist wrote that the Israeli government was involved in illegal organ trade. Jewish clergy organized a letter-writing campaign against him that got him fired. Eventually, a rabbi was arrested in New York and a Israeli military doctor was blamed but no apology to the journalist whose life they ruined. The military was harvesting organs not only from Palestinian prisoners but also from Israeli soldiers. You can read about it in the Jewish community press but if anyone else writes about the endemic corruption in their society they just turn nasty. Like Islamic fundamentalists, the rabbis hold Jewish communities under a tight grip and nobody can escape their wrath. I used to think that Islam had a strategic weakness because opportunists could easily exploit its strictness. Later, I learned that any religion or any grassroots movement is vulnerable and can be co-opted. Our strengths will be used against us. Buddhists in Sri Lanka and Burma had participated in the xenophobic policies against Hindu Tamils. That was an outcome of the longstanding British policy of favouring

Tamils for government jobs. The imperialists overlords did not trust the locals so they imported outsiders and showed them favouritism. In Iran, the British oil company favoured the Bahai minority. The globalists want divisions in society. If there is no division, they import outsiders and create new division. They foster conflict and ensure both sides fight. Even when the gruesome events have passed into history, the globalists try to sow division among new generations by forever reminding the young and impressionable about *past oppression*. That is why we as free men and women should be vigilant. In a dictatorship, it is the oppressors who need to be vigilant because they can be overthrown any time. In a democracy, the citizens need to be vigilant because their power can also be weakened by divisions or outsiders. The globalists are very dangerous and will spare no one. Even the Jews with all their wealth and power cannot stand up to them. The globalists financed Hitler and Mussolini. In those days, the globalists were known as internationalists. Before that, they were known as imperialists. It will all be clear to you if you read the books *Wall Street and the Bolshevik Revolution, Wall Street and the Rise of Hitler* and *National Suicide: Military Aid to the Soviet Union* by Andrew C. Sutton. In my school library, there was a book titled *How the Soviets steal America's hi-tech* or something. It said that the US government was secretly letting the Soviets steal US high technology... for decades while pretending to be engaged in a Cold War. Today, the globalists are importing Islamists into Western countries. The Saudi crown prince recently admitted that they were exporting Islamic fundamentalism only at the behest of Western governments. These Islamists are now burning up churches and synagogues but the governments won't take action. They need these fundamentalists to radicalize their Muslim citizens so they will go and fight their clandestine wars in Libya, Syria and Iraq... you know... to steal the oil. Nothing is beneath them. Anyway... I got distracted... the famous confrontation between the half-Jewish king Herod and the Sannhedrin, the court of the so-called elders, was on account of the fact that the King had convicted and hanged a highway robber. Ordinarily, it is not something you would spar with a king but the Sanhedrin did. The stock of the Jewish elite went into the ground after that. The temple was destroyed for the second time by the Romans. In 70 A.D., Jews were expelled from Palestine. One of two bands of Jews that were allowed to remain were early

Christians. This was the church led by James, the brother of Jesus."

"Oh, that is how Christianity started."

"No, this church was destroyed. James claimed that the new Christians, known as Gentiles by Christians and disparagingly as Goys by Jews, did not have to obey the old Jewish laws. He was stoned to death."

"What?"

"A Jew named Paul took over the church. He was initially involved in lobbying synagogue officials to persecute the new Gentiles but for some reason he decided that their Church should function alongside Jews or thrive elsewhere. He negotiated with the Jews and the Gentiles and tried to work out a live-and-let-live agreement. He was only partly successful. So, it was Paul who started Christianity proper."

"Why was he partly successful?"

"He was also stoned to death."

"What?"

"Don't worry. That is only what the Church claims. The Christian world remembers him as St. Paul. Some of his followers moved to Rome. In the 4th century, they somehow convinced the emperor Constantine to give the status of sole state religion to Christianity. The Roman empire was polytheistic until then. Their religion was much more civilized, liberal and tolerant. The records of the new Christians disparagingly refer them as *pagans*. The Western world wants everyone to think that their culture is a liberal Judeo-Christian culture. Nothing could be far from the truth. Judaism is a illiberal primitive religion. Christianity had formally denounced Judaism and split from it so the term Judeo-Christian is an oxymoron. Western culture can be considered liberal because the ancient pagan culture was liberal. This Roman emperor remained pagan until his death. On his deathbed, he was supposed to have converted to Christianity. Historians suspect that this conversion was a latter-day invention of the Church. However, after Christianity became official, this noble religion of love, peace and brotherhood started persecuting other religions. They destroyed pagan temples, monuments and even sacred groves and trees. They burned all pagan books and historical records they could find. Even non-religious books were burned. Europe officially entered the Dark Ages because of Christianity. Later, they wrote new history claiming that the pagans were uncivilized, practised witchcraft and performed human sacrifices. See how history repeats itself? Church leaders led violent Christian mobs who brutally killed and tortured prominent pagans including philosophers, scientists, priests and astrologers. Their favourite method of torture was believe-it-or-not crucifixion! The persecution of pagans continued for several centuries. During this time, traditional or pagan Roman holidays that could not be banned or suppressed were given a Christian colour. So-called Christian saints replaced Roman gods. The St. Valentine's Day was originally a Roman festival that just could not be eliminated."

"Valentines day is a Roman festival?"

"Even December 25 is a Roman holiday. The exact birth date of Jesus Christ is not known."

"So, Christianity is not really Christianity?"

"It is called Pauline Christianity. A lot of historical events were backdated and changed. The history and beliefs of other inhabitants were appropriated. New 'history' was written. If someone just goes by the Bible, he cannot not become a Christian. To be like Christ is to be Christian. Jesus Christ set an example to the world. Prophet Mohammed was also a reformer. Both of them tried to reform an ancient group of people with very primitive beliefs. Simple living and selfless service is their message."

"Not converting people?"

"No. There has to be a spiritual transformation for true acceptance. Conversion was an excuse for plundering. After the Muslim king Saladdin drove out Christians from Palestine, the Crusaders returned and started robbing their home countries. So, the pope sent them to parts of Europe that were not yet conquered by Christianity. That was how the Baltic regions now occupied by the countries Estonia, Latvia and Lithuania, the last strongholds of paganism, became Christian. When Europeans landed in Africa, Asia or the Americas, they were not plundering the foreign lands. They were civilizing." I said *civilizing* in air quotes. "Bringing God to the heathen. Of course, in those days, the American or African continents were sparsely populated. There were lots of tribes very isolated from each other or who fought each other. There were some kingdoms but they could not defend against European powers. The European imperialists justified their invasion and plundering by giving it a religious colour. Even today, the funds for religious conversion is not to spread religion. It is to cut the historical ties that binds a man to his people and his land. That is why we should not directly oppose foreign religions. We should oppose the sponsors of religious conversion. When a Christian preacher tries to sell his snake oil abroad, people should ask 'Why are you trying to preach Christianity to me? Go back to your country and preach there. Particularly, preach to the converted over there. They seem to need Christianity more than anyone here.' Now that the imperialists have spread out to all countries, they are suppressing even Christianity. In the US, you cannot to say 'Merry Christmas' because that is hurtful to Jews and Muslims. You must say 'Happy Holidays!' Christian money is fine if it is spent on trafficking illegal immigrants into the country but it is bad if it is spent on treating COVID patients."

"Trafficking illegal immigrants?"

"A lot of cash-rich Christian charities have been roped into picking up illegal immigrants at the Mexican border and shipping them deep into US mainland. You remember how an Indian diplomat was strip-searched in the US a few years back?"

"Yeah."

"It was a charade by the Obama government to show that they really took human trafficking as a serious crime. Bureaucrats in the American government stage these public-relations stunts once in a while to fool the public. They jailed cookbook writer Martha Stewart just to show that were tough on on insider trading. If they were really serious, Wall Street would grind to a halt. Hedge funds would lose all their profits. Small fry like Raj Rajaratnam get prosecuted but big Wall Street firms like Goldman Sachs get away with a fine. The British bank HSBC was revealed to have helped drug cartels, terrorists and countries under sanctions launder billions of dollars of money. Drug cartels were using special boxes that fit the exact dimensions of teller windows. Obama government let them off with a small fine and did not criminally prosecute any HSBC officials. Obama government also gave government weapons to a Mexican cartel. When this got leaked, the Obama government came up with the story that they were trying to track illegal guns. I am saying why should Americans give up their legal guns if their government is giving foreign criminals in their country with government guns."

"Why did their government object to treating COVID patients?"

"Yeah! When the epidemic started, New York City claimed that it was being overwhelmed with patients. A Christian charity put up medical treatment tents in Central Park. Some people complained that the charity held religious beliefs 'hateful' to homosexuals. The city administration sided with the outrage mob and asked the charity to close their tents. Neither of them could do any good but they prevented the ones who were helping. Christians cannot preach. Christians cannot stand in prayer. They cannot tell their kids what is good or bad. Even the American flag is now considered hateful because it makes foreigners less welcome."

"The American flag and its colours used to be cool. It was used on a lot of clothes and accessories."

"After Bush and Obama, USA represents the nation that bombs Third World countries and steals their oil. Previous American presidents would at least make some pretence. These two guys just threw away that veneer."

"Obama was a Nobel PEACE Prize winner."

"He received that even before he did anything as president. An honest man would have rejected it and said, 'Judge me after my term is over.' All he had done was make campaign promises and win an election. He gets the prize. It seems like a payoff."

"Like as a sign-up bonus."

"Exactly."

"There is a Steve Martin movie in which Eddie Murphy says that a Black man needs to get his ass whipped to get an Oscar nomination but a White man just needs to act stupid. You've seen the movie *Forrest Gump*?"

"Yeah. I've seen bits of that movie when I browse the channels and I have seen Tom Hanks acting stupid. I don't see sad slow boring movies. I've seen that Steve Martin movie... fully. It is called *Bowfinger*. America must have had a lot of improvement in race relations since that movie because Americans voted a second term for Obama even after they knew he was bad. How can these racist Americans make the same mistake twice in a row?" I shook my head in mock disbelief. "There is a speech that Obama gave before the UN General Assembly in which he states that his country will use all its military power against any country that comes between it and the oil in the Middle East. He stated that in the clearest manner possible. There was no mistaking what he said. No room for misinterpretation. Can a Black man serve Western imperialists any more than that? Some people had accused that because his father was a Kenyan and because he was not born in the US, he was not a real American."

"If he was really a Kenyan, he would not have bombed Africa."

"Exactly."

"How did Lincoln become a saint?"

"He was an opportunist. He was a mass-murderer who instituted the first concentration camps in the American continent... the camps interned not just combatants but also women and children, someone whose solution to Black slavery was to deport the semi-human negroes back to Africa... His life and history was given a complete makeover to brainwash generations of Americans. The greatest change that he introduced was the currency known as the greenback. It was issued without interest and was backed by the faith in the credit of the State, not by gold or private banks. He probably was assassinated because of that."

"Semi-human?"

"In those days, Blacks were not considered fully human, even when they had adopted Western names and religion..."

"There was a chapter in our English reader written by the famous boxer Mohammed Ali... he was then known as Cassius Clay... in which he complained that despite winning the Olympic gold for his country he was being repeatedly referred by his blackness, as if he was somehow lesser because of it. In a church sermon celebrating his win, they prayed for God to bless his *black soul*. He became very annoyed with that. Today, Blacks and Whites in America consider the word for the entire *negro* race to be a slur."

"Political correctness is born out of prejudice. When someone replaces the word *blind* with the word *visual disability*, they are only affirming their prejudice against physical handicaps. Political correctness is essentially a mask for hidden prejudice."

"Political correctness presumes guilt."

"Political correctness is a self-issued get-out-of-jail permit."

"Political correctness is meaning appropriation."

"Political correctness is not inclusive."

"Political correctness is defamatory."

"Political correctness is thought bullying."

"Political correctness is intolerant."

"Political correctness is weaponised negativity."

"Political correctness is toxic subjectivity."

"All this walking on eggshells does not stop the American entertainment industry from profiting from the use of the word *nigger*. They pay Black actors and singers to use the word and justify it as that is how Black people speak among themselves. They also claim that the word *nigga* with an *aa* at the end is different from the word *nigger*."

"Booker T said that the word should not be used."

"Booker T. Washington?"

"Booker T, the wrestler."

"Booker T was great. His scissor kicks and spinaroonie were great but his talent was never given a good run by the WWE."

"They give Roman Reigns or John Cena all the belts they want."

"They can be champions forever! Roman Reigns is a Samoan, I think. Umm … There is a company in Africa called Nigaz. It is a joint venture with the Russian Gazprom company and the Nigerian National Petroleum company. The name Nigaz is an amalgamation of their names. Some Americans took offence to that. The Nigerians themselves didn't care. They were happy that a foreign company has used the name of their country. If these Americans are to be believed, even the name Nigeria would have to be a slur. The audacity of Americans to disrespect an entire nation… It's unbelievable! American Blacks have been brainwashed. It is the result of the divide-and-rule policy of their ruling elites. Guilt-tripping the Whites and giving a persecution complex for the Blacks has become a national pastime. It is a distraction from the inability of the politicians to solve the actual problems affecting both groups as citizens of one country."

I paused and recollected my thoughts. Where was I? "Lincoln freed the slaves, not because he was such a good guy, he just wanted to hurt the Southern economy. The US colony of Liberia in Africa was created as the homeland for emancipated slaves. Today, they say there is no such thing as race."

"Caucasian, Mongoloid, Negroid, Aryan, Dravidian… these are not races?"

"No, they are 'social constructs,'" I said with air quotes. "The current thought is that even gender is a social construct. A man can claim to be a woman and he will be allowed to enter a women's toilet or hit the showers with them."

"What?"

"Obama brought that rule in schools. The US media, tech industry, Hollywood and even the United Nations supported him. Men are now competing in women's sports. There are numerous reports of male prisoners getting themselves transferred to female prisons and then assaulting the female inmates and even the female guards. A convict just has to put an elastic band in his hair and say, 'I am a woman now' and the jail authorities transfer him."

"That should be called gender appropriation!"

"If women want to call THIS an example of toxic masculinity, then they are right. The Olympics is allowing men to compete in women's sports. When they start stealing all the medals in more women's events, then other countries of the world will become aware of what is happening."

"How come the news reports don't mention the fact that men with gender-comprehension problems are entering women's bathrooms?"

"It is not just the men. Women are also removing their breasts."

"What?"

"It has got to do something with hormone disruptors in their diets. For decades, they have been using chemicals to improve meat and milk and egg production, and it must have had consequences. The media does not talk about it. Hospitals are exploiting pre-teen children and confused teenagers by performing castration surgeries and prescribing puberty blockers. A lot of these kids are now suffering from what is known as *transition regret*. The girls rue their lost breasts and hate their male voices. Instead of providing education, schools are promoting this kind of harmful propaganda. To protect the industry and the government from lawsuits, the media is setting one identity against another. Divide and rule. Don't let any crisis go to waste. That's their mantra. Indians don't know what happens in America and Americans don't know what happens abroad. Their media is conservative with truth and liberal with falsehood. All they care about is war, invading countries and stealing. They exist only to make more money for Wall Street. American wire agencies supply all the foreign news to India and other countries. They censor stuff that is embarrassing for them and they amplify stuff that is embarrassing to others. During Maha Kumbh Mela that happens once in 12 years, hordes of Western photographers descend on Varanasi to photograph naked sadhus smoking *ganja* and dead bodies being burnt at the ghats. They shock their readers with these photos and say, 'This is India'."

"Do you know why the sadhus are naked and why are they smoking ganja?"

"It is some obscure sect that does this. They picked up the ganja habit from Western photographers who came to the country in the 60s to photograph naked sadhus. They are unable to quit. They have become addicted. In some northern states, ganja is a cash crop like cotton. The painkiller and psychotropic drugs are essentially ganja.”

“Some years ago, I read a column by Ruskin Bond or some Anglo-Indian or some well-known writer or columnist who took offence about a photograph that a Western magazine or newspaper had published. It was of a female migrant labour sitting in a railway station. The caption under the photograph said that the woman was most likely pondering over the gloomy future as she suffers in abject poverty. The columnist had a different take. To him, she seemed like a content industrious woman who was looking forward to her new gig at the end of the journey.”

“Mark Twain said that a native's opinion about his country is not interesting. A foreigner's opinion of how the country struck him is more fascinating. Still, I think there has to be a difference between a tourist and a journalist. In my jokebook, I have covered this kind of dichotomy with an entire chapter on journalism.”

"Well, forget politics. It is frustrating. You said something about modern art. I know that it is not real art. How did it become respectable and in demand?"

"During the Cold War, Leftists started gaining influence in US academia. To counter that, the US government started the modern art craze. They invented something called 'American abstract expressionism' and paid a lot of journalists, professors, museum curators and art critics to rave about it. Like Feminism, it became wildly popular."

"Feminism is about women's freedom!"

"Feminism is about reducing or limiting the rise of the wages of the working class by bringing in women. During the world wars, American industrialists made huge profits by supplying war material to the government. During this time, the workforce was plagued by strikes and trade-unionism. The men struck work even when a war was going on. By reducing the wages of the workers, the owners could double or triple their profits. Women were to brought to work in factories because of the military draft but after the war the women would have to be made to stay. The men were too uppity. They tend to ask for wage increases, better work conditions and other benefits. In contrast, the women were just happy to have an independent source of income so they worked without complaints. They were 'emancipated.' Essentially, Feminism is another implementation of the divide-and-rule policy of the ruling classes. Of course, the woman was always at risk of getting pregnant, taking a break and never returning to the workforce. So, they tricked women into postponing marriage and children. Women were also tricked into believing that men were their enemies…"

"… when in reality?"

"… we love women. We do not meet in secret and conspire to oppress them."

"It just comes naturally?"

"It comes naturally. In a race, someone has to come first. Maybe men have to be more grateful but both sexes have to do their fair share. I believe that there is not much difference between men and women. There may be some difference but as Pepé Le Pew said 'Vive le difference'.

"Who is Pepe La?"

"The skunk in Bugs Bunny cartoons."

"Oh!" She got up and started hopping around me. "Hello, Cherie!"

"Madame, control yourself! Women can be crooked. They can kill. Women are the #1 reason for male mortality."

"Really?"

"After diseases and accidents. Most men who take their lives blame their wives. Behind every unsuccessful man too, there may be a woman."

"Can't men succeed on their own?"

"Yeah, it is a stupid idea! I am playing with words for the sake of rhetoric. The truth is we like women and we are not trying to drag you down. We wish the best for our womenfolk. Parents wants all their kids to be happy. In fact, they worry more about their female kids. This discrimination is not a problem for male kids because we have always wanted less attention from our parents. We don't want to be coddled. On the other hand, women have special reservation, discounts, buses, train compartments, seats…"

"Because, otherwise, your hands will be all over us."

"Yeah! The government would not have built the Aadhaar ID database if our fingerprints had been erased. Both men's and women's.

"Probably."

"Women have themselves to blame."

"How?"

"What has low life expectancy, poor hygiene, deficient vision, inadequate sense of direction, risk of going bald and high self-esteem?"

"What?"

"Men. What has high life expectancy, better hygiene, superior vision, adequate sense of direction, zero risk of going bald and low self-esteem?"

"Women? It's all our fault?"

"Yeah."

"Okay. Moving all that aside and returning to science fiction, is there anything you do believe in? I would like to read some REALISTIC sci-fi." She said 'realistic' with wide-open eyes.

"There is a lot of great fiction about time travel. You are supposed to have fun reading science fiction. You should not believe in the fancy ideas. *Invisible Man* is a fun concept. If he were to exist, he would be blind. A reflective surface has to exist in the eye to form an image so that the brain can understand it. For something to become transparent, the chemical compositions will have to change too. If that were to happen, then the person could not be human or living. Thus, science fiction has no practical use. Online classes and telecommuting may have been predicted in books decades ago but that was just casual speculation. When I was a kid, I knew that everyone today will be going around in flying cars. I bought my motorcycle a few years ago. It is still land-based. There have been… some exceptions."

"Oh, some science got through?"

"Geostationary satellites, for example. A science-fiction writer came up with the idea that the gravitational force could compensate for the centripetal force at the geostationary orbit. It made satellites that were placed at that distance seem like they were not moving at all, that is, from the perspective of the ground station. Why did Arthur C. Clarke have to invent that nonsense? Why didn't the shyentists who waste so much public money on non-existent particles come up with that idea?"

"So, authors are better than scientists?"

"Scientists are humans. Expertise in some field does not make you smart. You can't be smart all the time. Nobody can handle the pressure."

"You can tell knowledgeably."

"From personal experience? Yes, I can tell. We do not want the pressure." We both laughed. "Authors are certainly no better than scientists. Arthur C. Doyle who wrote the famous Sherlock Holmes stories was thought to be a super-intelligent man. In some ways, he was. However, he fell for a hoax created by two girls. The girls got into the papers after they used trick photography to create images of what they claimed were tiny fairies. Doyle did some research and claimed that the fairies were real. He did this in an article published in the same *Strand* magazine that made the Sherlock Holmes stories famous. There is some stuff that science cannot possibly explain. The width of the universe, for example. If they say the universe is only so big then that begs the question, 'What lies beyond it?'"

"You do seem annoyed by the high-science stuff?"

"I just don't see a good reason for so much fuss. It is the Mona Lisa effect all over again. There are some theoretical stuff such as the matter and anti-matter stuff that I do find interesting."

"What is that?"

"It is a theory about certain particles that are the exact opposite of known particles such as electrons, protons and neutrons. When an electron and anti-electron meet, they destroy each other. An anti-proton has the same mass as a proton but has negative charge. When they come together, they collapse into each other and destroy themselves. This is why the scientists say they are so rare… so imaginary."

"I'm glad you are not totally anti-science."

"Of course, not. Hey, have you heard of that joke about the neutron that walked into a bar?"

"The bartender said, 'For you, no charge'?"

"Do you know what happened after that?" She shook her head so I said, "A neutrino sitting nearby ordered a drink."

"And?"

"He thought he might also get a free drink."

"He didn't because?"

"Because, a neutrino, like an electron, has no weight."

"I should have known that. Any more gems like that in your joke book?"

"How many astronauts does it take to screw a light bulb?"

"And the answer is?"

"One to screw the bulb in but several to prevent the spacecraft from spinning in the same direction."

The Lift

I got this story from someone I met on a train. The rains had caused a landslide. Some boulders landed on the tracks and a train derailed. The railways is very efficient in these matters and they quickly restored the line. However, almost all passengers had cancelled their tickets or postponed their travel. I took this opportunity to book my ticket. Usually, I had to book one month in advance. This time, I was able to travel the very next day. On the train, there were very few passengers. In my coach, there were just a handful of people, at least in the beginning. A lift engineer got the seat opposite to me and we got talking.

"My father believes that ghosts exist because he had once met a woman who suddenly became mental and started speaking in a language that she had never spoken before."

"I have heard of incidents like that too. How can science or medicine explain something like that?"

"Oh, I was just saying that my father believed in ghosts. I don't believe in ghosts."

"You don't think the woman was possessed by a ghost? You do believe your father don't you?"

"Of course, I believe him. I don't think the woman was possessed by a ghost. She must have suffered a mental episode in which some stuff that was recorded in the deeper recesses of her brain was able to find voice. She could not have done it if she was fully conscious. She must not have had the ability to construct new sentences in that language. She heard someone speak in that language and repeated it from memory. That's all. I don't think she gained proficiency in that language."

"Well, that IS an explanation I have to admit. However, I can tell you a story from my personal experience that will give you some doubts."

"Okay, I would like to correct my earlier statement. I'm yet to come across a convincing ghost story. I'm willing to believe it if it is believable."

"So, I can tell you my story? A real story. You ready for it?"

"Sure, go ahead."

"Well, a few years ago, a night watchman died in one of our lifts. There was nothing wrong with the lift. It was working normally.

However, it had a manually operated steel door. If you are not careful, you will die."

"The collapsible door kind of lift?"

"Yes. I checked the electricals, electronics and the mechanical components of the lift from top to bottom and nothing was wrong. The top portion of the man was entirely crushed. The police wanted to investigate but there were elderly folk in the apartment complex and we had to put the lift back in service quickly. The post-mortem confirmed that the man had alcohol in his system but not enough to be drunk. While I was on assignment at the complex, a young man who lived alone in one of the flats asked me what we were doing. He then said he was thinking he might have caused the accident. I asked him what happened. Just then, somebody walked past us and he stopped talking. He left without saying what happened. A week later, he got my phone number from my company and called me. He wanted to speak to me in private. We had closed the case and so did the police and there was nothing more to do. Anyway, I asked him to meet me at a restaurant. He arrived there promptly."

"On the night of the accident, I was working on a DIY electronics project. I usually work on DC but this was an AC project. I don't have much experience with it. That night, I shorted the contacts of a circuit board and caused the fuse to trip. It was dark and I did not know what to do. I was afraid to get up lest I accidentally touch some live wire. After a while, the current came back. I think the watchman was in the lift when the current went out. When someone flipped the tripper back up, the lift must have moved again and crushed him."

"You are worried about nothing. The tripper affects only your flat or your floor. Someone might have switched it on because the lights were off. The flats and the lift are on different supply lines. A short-circuit in one flat will not affect the lift. You will have to press a switch to make a stalled lift move again."

"Well, I'm relieved to hear that but there are other problems."

"What problems?"

"I think the dead man's ghost is in the lift."

"What makes you think that's the case?"

"A few days after your men had left, I took the lift with my girlfriend. We were planning to go to a movie."

"And?"

"The lift stopped and became pitch-dark. My girlfriend screamed suddenly. The lights came back after a while. I asked why she had screamed but she just slapped me in the face. She said I tried to grab her hand. I didn't do anything."

"People imagine things when they are afraid."

"That's not all."

"What else?"

"My girlfriend went back to her place and I had to return to my flat. I did not want to take the lift so I took the stairs."

"And?"

"When I reached the first floor, I heard the lift come up. I saw its light come up and I heard its bell chime. There was nobody in the lift and no one was waiting for it. I took the next set of stairs. Behind me, I heard the lift move up and when I was on the second floor, the lift was waiting for me. I was too afraid to look if anyone was there in it. So, I ran past the third set of stairs. The lift followed me there too. This time I summoned courage and looked. No one was there inside or outside the lift. For the next two floors, I ran up the stairs without stopping but the lift was waiting for me when I reached my floor."

"Have you gone crazy or did these things really happen?"

"I was thinking the same thing too. So, the next day, I waited for someone to walk the stairs with me. Some people in the first few floors take the stairs all the time but never the lift."

"And what happened?"

"I followed a lady to the third floor and she noticed it too. She thought it was strange but she was not scared like me."

"So, you are saying that when you go to your floor, the lift follows you?"

"Yes."

"Are you sure?"

"Definitely."

"Okay, let's go and check it out."

"Did it follow him?"

"Sure, it did."

"It only happened in the evening during the watchman's duty hours. I replaced the circuit boards and it stopped following him… for a few days. After that, it moved only when he was alone. However, I could see from outside the building that the lift was following him."

"So, did this phenomenon stop or is still following him? Did he finally move out?"

"The watchman was very poor and had no relatives with him. He was buried without any final rites. Labour contractors hire very old homeless or abandoned men for these jobs. They give them the lowest possible salaries. The watchmen live on practically nothing. In life, they have absolutely nothing to look forward too. They usually live under the stairs with just a sheet of cloth for privacy. His daughter lived in another state and did not know he had died. She is also very poor. The boy consulted a priest and performed the dead man's final rites. He even performed a *shatru samhara homam.* The haunting issues got over after the final rites were performed but he decided to do the homam just to be sure. He cannot move out of the complex because his parents had given the flat to him."

"And the lift stopped following him?"

"Yes. I didn't do anything to the lift. There was nothing wrong with the lift."

"Well, I don't know what to say."

"Well, I say, 'good night and sweet dreams'."

Early next morning, I arrived at my apartment complex from the railway station. The lift came to the ground floor but there was no one in it. Maybe someone pressed the button and then instead of waiting decided to take the stairs. I did too, purely for health reasons.

"After hearing these scary stories, my kids are not going sleep tonight."

"I can tell some funny stories that will erase everything."

"That will be great."

"Well… A Russian, an American, an Indian and a Pakistani were travelling in a plane. Suddenly, the pilot announces that the plane is running out of fuel and all passengers should ditch their baggage to reduce the load on the plane. The Russian says, 'The Soviet Union is the world's largest producer of diamonds and I don't need this big bag of diamonds,' and kicks it out of the door. The American says, 'The USA is the richest country in the world and I don't need all this gold.' He then opens a suitcase full of gold and heaves it out of the door. Now, it's the Indian's turn because the Pakistani is still sleeping. The Indian has nothing valuable or heavy so he pushes the Pakistani passenger out of the door."

The kids liked this story. Vampira has been trying not to laugh at my jokes but I see signs of her reserve breaking down.

"Another story like that? A Russian, an American and an Indian are circling around the earth in an international space station that has gone out of control. As the craft is drifting around the earth, the American astronaut puts his hand out of the window to see what was happening. After a while, he yells and yanks his hand inside. 'We are flying over New York. I know because one of the tall buildings there just scraped my hand.' The Russian cosmonaut puts his hand out of the window and after a while brings it back in with a yell. 'We are flying over Russia. One of our Soviet rockets just flew by and singed my hand. We send so many of them into space.' This causes a stalemate and they both look at the Indian. The Indian does not have much hope but out of modesty he puts his hand out of the window. After a while, he also lets out an yell and withdraws his hand. The Indian says, 'I guess we are flying over India.' The Russian and American are puzzled and ask him how he came to that conclusion. The Indian replies, 'A few minutes after I put my hand out, I decided to check the time and I found that my watch had gone missing.'"

This time, Vampira let go and was holding her face in her palms. "Victory is yours!" I told myself.

"How about one more story like that? Well, there was international conference for police officers. In one informal group, the discussion went like this. A British bobby says, 'There is no case that the Scotland Yard cannot solve.' Then, a Russian policeman says, 'In

Soviet Russia, the crime rate is very low because Socialism provides for everyone according to his need. And, if despite that, there is some crime or dispute, the *militsiya* will solve it in half an hour.' After that an American cop said, 'In the USA, the police will reach the trouble spot within 10 minutes of the first emergency phone call.' Finally, an Indian policeman got to speak. 'In India, the police knows about any crime even before it is committed.'

Vampira is still laughing.

"Now, we can forget about these jokes too. How about a brain teaser? Can you say 100 words in 60 seconds but none of the words can have the letters A, B, C or D?"

Lots of thinking and false-starts.

"Stop wracking your brains. I will give you the answer. Zero, one, two, three, four, five, six and so on until ninety-nine"

"These numbers don't have the letters ABCD?"

"No!"

After some cajoling and threatening, the kids left with their mother.

Femme Fatale

The money from the exorcism lasted quite a while but inevitably I was back to living on scraps. Fortunately, a friend of a friend of a friend called me to the City. Apparently, they had bought a video rental place to whitewash some black money on some benami property bought using the hawala route. I did not have to understand the details. All that I had to do was to give the business a boost and make sure that it was a going concern — for tax purposes. They were just putting up a front.

While most people stream movies, video rentals still has takers in NYC. Even a niche market can be a big market in a big cosmopolitan city such as this. The pretend owners of the store, for the life of them, could not drum up any business. Not one customer had gone past their doors after the store had opened. Most of the videos were tapes. Not DVDs.

For over a week, I spent time on several online pallet auctions for some good deals for DVDs. I made a few small purchases but I really hit jackpot when I won a consignment of Funai VCRs. These were the last VCRs made in Japan. They got lost in shipping and was stuck in a warehouse for six years. I got two hundred VCRs for around $400. I then spent $100 to get these checked and working in good condition. They all were. Next, I printed leaflets for the ITALO MUSIC & VIDEO HOUSE club offering a free collectible Japanese VCR for the first 150 members. Only $50 for a whole year and get 12 movies free! I then distributed the leaflets outside cinemas hosting a film festival.

Back at the store, customers started trickling in. Memberships were being bought and VCRs were disappearing. I recouped all the money I spent on the VCRs from the subscriptions. After a week, there was a customer or two at any time of the day. This however was not sustainable so I moved to Phase 2.

One day, a female professor from a nearby journalism school came in.

"Hi, I'm looking for some inspirational movies with journalists in the lead doing some real hardcore reporting."

"Well, there is *Switching Channels* with Kathleen Turner. It is more of a comedy than anything. There is *Brenda Starr* with Brooke Shields. It is a fantasy film... If you want a real... realistic story about journalists..."

"Yes…"

"What you need is the 1988 Japanese movie *Evil Dead Trap*. It is about a… Is it all right if it is a foreign movie?"

"Oh, totally. If the movie has English subtitles, then it is fine."

"Oh, all our foreign movies are subtitled. This one is too."

"Great!"

"This movie is about a young ambitious female late-night talk-show host. She is known for her daring assignments. She does not care what politician or what megacorporation she is going to expose. She just goes out, digs up some dirt and shines the light of justice on their evil deeds. So, some of these evil fellows conspire to teach her a lesson by luring her to what they hope will be her last and final story. How she and her team survives and also exposes the culprits behind the plot is the remainder of the movie. There is a lot of action, very very very realistically done. There are no fake or corny dialogues that will embarrass real journalists."

"Sounds really exciting. I will definitely take it and show it to my class."

After her, a born-again Christian came in.

"I'm a born-again Christian and I would like a movie that will reinforce my faith in Jesus Christ."

"Well, we have a good collection of faith-based movies. The problem is they are all alike. If you have seen one, you have seen them all. But, if you want something that is entertaining and faith-affirming, then I suggest you see this movie."

I then showed him the 1991 movie *Nudist Colony Of The Dead*. His eyebrows vanished above his head.

"Even though the title says *Nudist Colony*, there is no nudity in this movie. It was created by a Christian director who put his own money in the project and hoped to bring the message of God to the gullible masses corrupted by Hollywood. Unfortunately, the religious folks ignored it because of the word 'nudist'. The Liberals disparaged it because of the zombies reform themselves and go back to their graves. The zombies were attacking a team of Christian campers who remain true to their faith."

"Seems promising. Are you sure there is no nudity in this film?"

"Well, even in a Christian adaptation of *Adam & Eve*, you will see some skin. But, in this movie, there is absolutely nothing. No nudity. Everyone remains fully dressed. The alleged nudist zombies are all covered with dirt, leaves, decaying clothes and putrefaction. In every scene, there is someone quoting the Bible. They also sing some really good hummable songs in the movie. The one that I remember are *God's gonna show us the way.*"

"Fine. I will take it."

Next, a person whom I could not identify as a boy or as a girl came in.

"Hello there. I'm going through some serious life changes now. Do you have some movie that I can relate with?"

"Sure. How about this movie? *Sleepaway Camp?*"

"What is it about?"

"Well, it is about a shy girl who goes to a teen camp. Several kids bully her. Her brother usually saves her from trouble but he cannot be with her all the time. She then becomes friends with a boy who accepts her as she is. I don't want to give away the ending but it is very memorable."

"Super-exciting! Thanks. I will borrow this one."

I sold tapes in this way all day that day.

Next day, I did not open the store. Shutters were still down when the protesters arrived and blocked the street. Local and national TV network crews visited the place. Everyone was surprised that evengelicals, alphabeticals and journalisticles would come together in a protest. After a few days, I asked someone to paste a huge notice on behalf of the new management apologising to everyone. The immigrant family, which had poured in all their savings and bought out the business, will be giving the offended customers a full refund or an extra year's membership for free. The protests disappeared overnight. The name of the shop was changed to *Falafel Video Shop.* The fake owners had to hire a Druze to manage the counter.

I got a fat envelope with 100-dollar bills for my troubles.

I reached my place and tried to find my key. My girlfriend of two

weeks sleeps most of the time and does not close the door or secure
the place in any way. I have not had any break-ins but it is a poor
neighbourhood. As I neared the door, I heard weird sounds. I
unlocked the door and went in.

"What happened to you?"

For the last few hours, she has been changing from a wolf to the
angel that she was and back again. Slowly at first. Now, very quickly.
It/she was on the floor all the time and trying to adjusting to the new
form.

I had my stick ready but was feeling drowsy. Suddenly, there was
a growl and the wolf sprung forward and flew in the air towards me.
At the last moment, I swung my stick with all my might. Before I fell
to the ground, I think I hit the wolf in the guts. I heard a whelp and
then silence. As I stood up, I looked around the room. The wolf had
disappeared. I looked up and in all the potential hiding places. I
couldn't find it. It was probably waiting for me outside so I did not
venture there.

After waiting half an hour, I set the table for dinner. When I was
eating, she walked in. There was a reddish welt around her belly. The
rest of her was splendid as usual. She was not dressed for dinner yet
she sat at the other side of the table.

"You are not allowed at the table."

"But, you said I was your girlfriend forever!"

"No dog is my girlfriend!"

I took my stick and slammed it on the table. She transformed
into the wolf, slinked out of the chair and walked out of the room
with its tail between its legs.

I finished my dinner. Then, I found a plastic plate and put the
reminder from my dinner and leftovers in it. I placed the plate and
bowl of water in the verandah and closed the door. Then, I went to
sleep.

Next morning, as I was preparing for business, I heard her again.
She walked up to the door and just stood there.

"Will you stop standing naked at the door? I have some customers coming in today. One look at your big fat butt and they are gone forever."

She walked in and looked at herself in the mirror.

"Do you think I look fat?" she asked.

"No, it's the mirror that's looks small."

She seethed in anger.

"Okay, the mirror adds 200 pounds."

She walked out. I thought of other quips like that.

"The circus called and the elephant wants its dress back. Wait, she is not wearing any clothes. Who cares? The Statue of Liberty called. She wants her clothes back. Why did the werewolf couple break up? They broke up because what he brought home was just dogfood. Why did the vampire couple break up? They broke up because she left him emotionally drained. No, they broke up because he gave her low blood pressure and she gave him high blood pressure. No, no. They broke up because he did not want to be caught dead with her. Why did the zombie couple break up? They broke up because he was always buried in work."

I laughed and laughed and laughed. Then, I realized that that's how the symptoms start. Laughing at my own jokes. Believing the stuff is funny. It's the onset of delusional mental disease. It's an occupational hazard. "Symptoms, my friend!" I warned myself.

I then wondered where she went. There was some movement in my peripheral vision. The wolf was standing on the beam above. Then, it jumped. Midway, it transformed into her fat self and pinned me down like a truck on a motorcycle. This is how it is going to end, I realized. It's all over now.

"Are you going to kill me?" I said as we struggled.

"You said you loved me and you changed your mind!"

"Yeah, that was before you decided to become a pack animal."

She pressed hard and I could not breathe. I tried to bring one leg up between her and me. No luck. She added more weight to my neck. I then realized I need to find thinner women. Thin and healthy. Panting, booty-shaking, licking, scratching … WARNING SIGNS! I don't how I'm going to euthanise this creature. Illegal immigration. Hate crimes. Racketeering. Bestiality. Murder. My rap sheet in this country is getting as big as the one in my home country. And, so quickly!

I brought both legs up and hoisted her up into the air. She landed a few feet next to me. She coughed as the wind got knocked out of her lungs. I got up and kicked her. It is true that we loved each other but I am afraid some irreconcilable differences have cropped up. I then rolled her over with my feet. I got on her back, twisted her hand behind her and pinned her neck down.

"Go ahead, bitch! Who sent you here?"

No response. Just more struggle.

I knee-kicked her in the small of the back.

"Talk!"

"I'm the only one who can save you. If you kill me, you will be killed too."

"Who sent you?"

"The woman who you tried to kill."

"I have killed several women. I have tried to kill even more. Which one?" Of course, I was bluffing.

"You are bluffing."

"Which woman?"

"The woman you tried to kill at the Philomel Cottage."

"Mademoiselle Zuma?"

"She sent me to kill you. I decided to protect you instead."

"Zuma is dead or left town. I've been getting her customers for weeks. Say the truth."

"All right. I'm Zuma. Can we both get along?"

"And bygones be bygones?"

"Bygones be bygones."

"What's with the four-legged *Animal Planet* action?"

"That's a wolf spirit I summoned to help me."

"Can you get rid of it?"

"Yes, it is a friendly animal spirit."

"Yes, very friendly."

Well, we are married now. We went into business together. No more fighting for scraps. She does palm-reading and horoscopes. I do Vastu Shastra. I don't do Vastu remedies. It is all right to do everything as per Vastu on some new construction but to demolish or alter an existing building is not my thing. No matter how great Vastu is, this is a foreign country. You can do everything 100% Vastu but if your fate is to be run over by an 18-wheeler, Vastu is not going to stop it. Vastu is more of a peace-of-mind thing and it should be economical. With the exorcism, I had no choice. I had to try everything.

The horoscopes line is done entirely using computer software. She just interprets the results. Her palm-reading and crystal-ball gazing was pure fraud. I got her a book of Kerala palmistry science and made her learn it. It was not easy. She preferred to make wild guesses and fool customers. I forced her to just read the palm and match it with suggestions in the book. If a guy has more aptitude, say, for finance and if he is digging ditches instead, she just says that he would have made more money if he had chosen a career in finance. We do not give false hopes. I hope people trust us because we are honest. I don't do exorcisms any more. I don't want to dabble in evil spirits.

I am trying to start a family with Zuma. I preferred the fatangel but as Johnny Bravo once said, "Four-legged dames are nothing but trouble." My wife is in the kitchen but she is laughing now. She thinks she can read minds. I convinced her that this ability offers no advantage in predicting the future for our customers.

The bottom line is no more fatangel. She is gone forever. Zuma is pretty but somewhat old and not as attractive.

"You are lucky you have me."

I will test her for a few years and then have a baby with her. I am afraid that one day when I come home, she will be howling at the moon. She is laughing and howling now.

"If you wait a few more years, our kid will be born with autism or Down's syndrome." She maybe right so I might change my mind.

By the way, if you are building a new house, get it built according to the principles of Vastu Shastra. It does not matter what religion you belong to. This is just a collection of time-tested building architectural principles to take advantage of nature. It may have been written around some religious identity but its precepts are practical and secular. Read my book on the subject and draw your own plans.

Zuma initially assumed that the place we were staying was abandoned property. From the outside, it does look like that. The inside is quite different. I need a good hideout and this place does fine for me as it is now. I do not want it to attract any attention.

When Zuma learned that the place was a rental, she wanted the whole place cleaned up. That is, only the outside. The inside is always clinically clean. She started nagging me to clear the space around the house. She wanted to plant a garden! I was not interested. I like to do the bare minimum to survive. Except for my daily morning exercise, I avoid all other forms of physical exertion. I am not going to slave in the dirt to grow crotons. It was not going to happen. After a few months avoiding the work, she tells me we can save money from the vegetables that will be growing in our garden. What?!!! That changes everything. Times are not always good. Why didn't she say this in the beginning? For a mindreader, she is not very perceptive.

I borrowed some tools from the junkyard behind us and brought them in a wheelbarrow to the front of the house. It was going to be a long day in the Sun. This is not a problem. I can work all day without breaking a sweat. If I were doing hard labour in prison, I would be smug as a bug in a rug. If it wasn't for the reports of rampant ass-raping, I would go there just for the work. Like in software and electronics, I decided to do a prototype or proof-of-concept garden first.

Before I moved in, I stayed at the junkyard for a few weeks. I fixed the roof (which had caved in) and the floor (which had almost disappeared). I had also replaced a few doors and windows. I did all this myself. A few days after I made the place liveable, the owner showed up. I think the junkyard man informed her.

This person was a rich old lady who owned several apartment buildings in the City. My house was where she was born and raised. She had given all her real estate holdings to her two sparring sons. This house was the only property that she still owned. The plot that the house stood on and the junkyard behind us were granted to her grandfather and a few other port workers by the State. After a flood, the river altered its course and a no-man's land was created. Her grandfather and a few workers of the State had appealed to the governor to give them the land. The governor acceded to their wish on the condition that the State was not responsible if the river changed course again. Most of the grantees had sold their lots to her grandfather and another man. That other man's descendant lives in the junkyard now.

The City tried to forcibly acquire the land several times and her father and later herself had to go to court each time to win it back. Out of spite, the City built an elevated road effectively isolating this land parcel from the rest of the city. They also refused to provide any kind of new commercial permits or building development plans, residential or non-residential. The City wanted them to sell the place to them or go to Hell. The property was now faced with Hell (the elevated road) on one side and high water (the river) on the other. The old house fell into disrepair. Her sons were not interested in maintaining it. She became immobile for a few decades after an accident. She made a visit once a year to lay flowers on the graves of her father, grandfather and a few of her old-time friends. Yes, I now realise that I am surrounded by dead people and when the *Zombie Apocalypse* happens this place could see some action.

The old woman seemed surprised to see me living there. She was even more surprised when she saw how I had fixed up the place. She let me continue to stay there, which I thought was very sweet of her until she said I have to now pay rent.

I had finished digging when a car pulled up at the gate. A middle-aged guy waved to me and stepped out. He introduced himself and we shook hands. After some talk about who recommended him to me, he said his wife had become brainwashed by a White spiritual 'guru'. This guru conducts online courses helping other 'spiritual beings' to 'transcend' themselves. Whatever that means. This man's wife had already spent $2000 for the courses and has been pestering him for more money. I did some digging online. This spiritual guide has a video channel with a few thousand subscribers. She talks about ancient civilizations and aliens from other universes including greys, Anunnakis and Plædians. I posted this message on her latest video.

> This lady has been making videos since 2011, perhaps longer. If she knows so much about the Plædians, she should be an ascended being now.

To which, she replied:

> I have been making videos since around 2008-09. You do not have to be ascended to speak about galactic connections with Plædians or any other beings. We have the capacity to understand them right now.

To that, I replied:

> The next time, you see or talk to an alien, take a picture and post it here. Thx.

For which, she replied:

> K. Will do.

I told the man to find a new young lawyer (to limit the fees) and send a legal notice. Specifically, he should warn the fraudster about making false claims and the penalties involved. A month later, the man called to say that he got his money back. I did not ask for any payment for the advice because the whole thing was worth a laugh.

UNLIKELY
STORIES

The
Seance

Zuma routinely eavesdrops on my thoughts but I always stay out of her side of the business. So, it was a surprise when she asked me to help with a client. This was a girl who was staying with a family as a paying guest. Lately, she has been encountering some strange experiences with her computer.

Her landlady was a widow. She rented out a room because she felt very lonely. The girl had almost the entire house for herself and was feeling elated at having landed such a fine place to stay for almost no money.

A few days after moving, she had a strange experience that followed a nightmare. In the dream, she was lying in bed when she saw a strange ball of light floating above her. It moved like a jellyfish drifting in the current. She tried to touch it but could not move her hands. With great difficulty, she raised her hands but the light moved further away. She tried to get up but her body felt anchored to her bed. She could not even turn her head. Subsequently, even her hands became senseless. She was totally paralysed. The light continued to grow bigger and got stuck to the false ceiling. It was now blinking like a star beckoning her. Again, with great difficulty, she raised her hands to grab it. A hooded skeleton grabbed her hands and pulled her up. Just then, she woke up from her sleep and found herself sitting on her bed. The skeleton had disappeared. But, the light which still remained floated across the room. It seemed to lose its

radiance as it moved. It finally disappeared over her table. On the
table, her computer seemed to be on. She thought maybe she forgot
to shut it down.

The next night, she had the same nightmare with the hooded
skeleton. She found herself sitting on the bed when she woke up. The
strange light from her dream moved and disappeared over her laptop.
This time, the laptop was shut down but not powered down. The LED
power indicator was still on. She tried hard but could not remember
if she had switched off power to the laptop.

The girl strongly believed that she was 'spiritual'. She came to
see Zuma for an explanation of her dreams. I could have asked her to
jump in the ocean but Zuma indulges these nutsos.

Zuma called me to her room. "Check this laptop and fix it if there
is any problem."

I opened the back of the laptop.

"This has the hard disk."

"Yes."

"You want me to check it?"

"Yes."

"Have you taken a backup of the data?"

"No."

"You should not give your laptop to someone with the hard
disk... with your data."

"What should I do?"

"Does the hard disk have any personal stuff?"

"Yeah, lots of photos and videos and some work documents."

I put the back cover on and placed the laptop on the table. I
switched it on and asked her to log in. There was a ton of startup
programs and browser add-ons. An unknown antivirus program was
also running. I could not disable or uninstall this anti-virus program. I
booted the computer using a USB disk drive with a Linux OS on it.
This Linux OS was customized by a popular antivirus vendor for
checking infected computers. After booting up, I ran the anti-virus
scan and it found a lot of spyware/malware programs, that is, not

including Windows and Chrome. I told the girl that the OS was compromised and that she will have to reinstall it and her software programs. Did she have any other programs other than Office? Lots of games, apparently. I said the games were the problem. She said she didn't care and that I could get rid of them. So, I backed up her data, in front of her, to an old hard disk that I had. Then, I repartitioned her hard disk. I installed the OEM Windows OS, drivers and the Office suite on a much smaller partition while the girl narrated her story in full detail. I also installed Ubuntu Linux on another partition in case Windows became sick again. I copied back her files from my hard disk to a separate partition. This partition was data-only and encrypted. I let the girl choose the password and passphrase. I shredded all the data from my hard disk in front of her, that is, except for her amazing collection of pirated old movies, which she generously shared with me. I did a cursory check of the hardware and everything seemed fine. Zuma had by now managed to get the girl to regurgitate her entire life history and was now beginning to speculate on the dream.

"Why don't we put a camera in her room and see what happens?"

"I doubt that will show anything," said Zuma.

"No harm in trying."

"Do you have a camera?"

I grabbed all my stuff that I had brought into the room and took them back to my room. When I returned to Zuma's room again, I had brought a camera for the girl.

"This is a battery-powered night-vision camera recorder. It has this superfast high-capacity memory card. The card is very cheap now but I paid a high price when it was released so do not lose it or damage it. Bring everything back safely tomorrow. Place the camera in some corner of the room that has a full view of where you are sleeping and where the laptop bag is placed."

That night, the girl had the same nightmare. She saw the mysterious light again. This was not captured on the camera. According to her, the light moved across the room and disappeared over to cupboard where the laptop bag was kept. The camera did record her becoming uneasy over her bed, waking up and walking over to the cupboard.

"This will need a seance."

"You mean we will need to hold our hands and speak to dead souls?"

"Yes but first you must get permission from your landlady."

The girl went back and spoke with her landlady. She phoned back to tell Zuma that the landlady was more than willing to meet Zuma. I've never taken part in a seance. Zuma has been a lot of fun before and after marrying her. Zuma smiled at me, placed the phone down and went back to her room.

In the evening, just before sunset, we took a taxi to the girl's address. It was in a better part of the town. The house was big but had no upper floors. The landlady opened the door and the girl was behind her. The house looked much better on the inside. We spent some time on small talk. The landlady did all the work herself. Some company took care of the lawns. Her husband died a year ago from cancer. She had no relatives except for an estranged son. She had no contact with him and did not know where he was.

Zuma suggested that the landlady also take part in the seance.

"Don't worry. Nothing will happen to you."

"I want to help. It is not a problem."

We closed all the doors and windows. We switched off all the lights, even those outside. I brought a table from the hall into the girl's room. I also brought in chairs for all of sit around the table. Now, I understood why Zuma asked me to accompany her.

Zuma placed a lamp on the table and lit it. She then placed a glass hood around the lamp. "Please sit down." I sat between Zuma and the landlady. The girl was opposite me. Zuma looked at the lamp and said, "Everyone, join your hands. Just listen to me and do what I say. Close your eyes. Clear your minds. Stop your thinking." Zuma then started whispering something… something I can only describe as nonsense. Zuma unclasped my hand and pinched me on the thigh. She again joined hands with me and continued with her whisperings in the… as-yet unidentified lingo.

The air in the room suddenly felt chilly even though the heater was on. I felt slightly dizzy. This was very unusual. Even when I drank alcohol, which I did a few times in my late twenties, I did not feel dizzy. Now, I felt the ground was somewhat shaking like a boat. I opened my eyes. The light had disappeared. There was no other light source. The walls of the room had disappeared. The table was there and the chairs were there. There was nothing above us or below us. Just darkness. Somehow, whatever I could see was lit by some sort of ambient lighting. I was still holding hands with the landlady who still had her eyes shut. I turned to Zuma. She was gone. There was a hooded person in her place. I could not see a face inside the hood. This person was taller than Zuma and gripped my hand much more firmly. I however could not see this person's hand. The girl opened her eyes and screamed. The landlady opened her eyes and moved back in her chair. She fainted and fell down. Her eyes were still half-open.

"I capital. L capital. Small O, V, E. ✶ capital. Small ✶, ✶, ✶, ✶, ✶, ✶."

The hooded figure then disappeared. The lamp reappeared. Zuma was back in her chair. The walls of the room came into view again. The ground became steady. My head hurt like I had seen a 3D movie.

"How many movies did you see from her hard disk?"

"Six. Seven, maybe."

"Help the old lady get back to her senses."

Zuma got up and blew out the lamp. The girl seemed like a deer caught in the headlights of a car. Zuma gently tapped her on the shoulder to wake her up.

The girl said she saw the skeleton or its skull inside the hood. The landlady claimed she saw her dead husband instead. He looked the same as the day before he died. '✶✶✶✶✶✶' was her name. I assumed that 'ILove✶✶✶✶✶✶' was the password to a computer or an email account.

The landlady could not access her husband's home laptop after he died. When she gave his laptop to me, it had not been charged for over a year. The battery was dead. The BIOS battery was also dead. I manually set the date and started the device with its AC brick.

I checked his email and found that he was in communication with a doctor who was treating his son. His son was suffering from 'post-traumatic stress disorder' that he acquired after a 'tour' abroad. He was in the US military and was later discharged with 'disability'. His real disability was illicit drugs and he had at one time tried to kill himself with them. The father had engaged a detective agency who tracked down his son to a veterans facility in the South. He probably did not tell his wife to spare her the bad news. When he fell ill and went into a coma, his secret died with him.

The next day, the landlady contacted the doctor. After a few months, she brought her son home to live with her. The girl meanwhile left to live in another place. Zuma did not give me any money for my contribution. She said the whole episode was quality entertainment and if I was not satisfied I could see those pirated movies as much as I wanted.

The Shapeshifter

I don't know how Zuma gets her clients. I advertise in local newspapers and I am lucky if I get two or three clients in a week. Zuma's day is filled with multiple engagements. Women seek her advice from far and afar. She listens to them patiently and they implicitly trust her. I don't know how she does it. Listening to people with problems is not my thing. Everything I know for earning a living leaves a paper trail. How can I stay under the radar and still make money? If a customer is not motivated himself, I do not impress upon him. 'Follow my advice or go to hell!' That is my general attitude.

I was bored to the depths when one day Zuma called me to her room. A young woman had driven over a hundred miles to see her. She was newly married. A snake was giving her trouble. I hate almost all critters. I kill them if I see them. Zuma is the opposite. She likes all animals. She is a vegetarian but she is not crazy like the vegans. This is fine because I do not eat beef or pork or mutton. I taught Zuma how to cook Indian meals and now she serves my kind of food every day. This marriage is a match made in heaven.

It was a surprise when Zuma seemed to ask me to get rid of a snake. "You want me to kill a snake?"

Every night, the young woman became knocked out of her senses at night. During this time, she has a nightmare involving a snake. All that she can recall is a snake crawling over her naked body and she being powerless to get rid of it. This snake was similar to a snake that was caught by the family that she was working for. She did tell them the snake was giving her nightmares but they laughed it off. She lived in a rural area and her pay was above average. Her work as a nurse was light and she did not want to quit. Her recent marriage was on the rocks now because she passes out each night.

"We will have to visit your place to see what is happening."

Zuma cancelled her appointments for the next few days and we packed an overnight bag. The young woman drove us to her place. Her husband opened the door. He had prepared a dinner for us.

After we ate and the dishes were cleaned, Zuma asked the two to go to their bedroom like usual while we waited outside. The man was supposed to let us know when his wife logged out of consciousness. This happened almost as soon as she slipped under the sheets. Her husband took us inside their bedroom. The woman's eyes were wide open and her husband closed them. I looked at Zuma. She asked us both to leave the room. We went outside but left the door just a bit to see what was happening.

Zuma took an urn out of her bag. She put something in it and lit a fire. She fanned it and the room was filled with smoke. In the smoke, I saw a thin girl with dark skin and strange clothing. The smoke made her visible. The girl had the blackest of black skins that I had ever seen. Because we were holding the door more widely open, the smoke was escaping and she was not fully visible. From what I saw, the girl seemed to have the most amazing features. They were not the kind you see on ordinary everyday people. Her body was like… how do I describe it… it was like… Zuma got up and closed the door on us. We both put our ears on the door and tried to listen to what was happening inside. Zuma and the girl were speaking in a strange language. After some back and forth, there was silence. Zuma opened the door and came out. She held the urn in one hand and her bag in the other. There was something heavy in the bag. The dark girl was gone. The young woman was regaining consciousness. Her husband went and sat beside her.

"What's in the bag?"

"I will tell you later."

"Is it the snake?"

"Mmmmm."

We waited for the couple to come out of their bedroom.

When they sat down with us, Zuma spoke. "The snake will not bother you anymore, at least for a few more months. You should quit this job immediately. If they are going to continue with hunting and you remain vulnerable to animal spirits, things may not turn out very well. Animal spirits are not very bright and can be indiscriminate. They may drive you to kill yourself. Take your time and let us know when you quit the job."

The woman quit the same week. A few months later, Zuma asked me to get the snake from the woman's employer house. On my first trip to their town, I reconnoitered the compound using a drone for a few days. The owner had two huge dogs. They were let out into the grounds during the night to guard the place. There were several CCTV cameras all over the property. They were all facing down. Still, I added camouflage decals to the drone. At night, large areas around the house were lit by IR cameras. I don't think there were any motion detectors because the dogs were running all over the place and they set off no alarms.

Electricity supply was brought to the house by an overhead service wire. It went to a room where the side entrance was located. There were several battery generators to provide redundant power to the house.

Some distance from the side entrance was a private zoo. It was supplied power by an underground wire. This place also had CCTV cameras.

One night, on my second trip, I noticed several cars leaving the property. I did not see anyone in the house or in the grounds. The dogs were locked inside the house. I decided this was a good time to test the CCTV cameras. I blackened my face and put on a mask. I climbed the street pole and disconnected the service wire. The house was plunged into darkness but some lights remained on. I crossed the fence and walked over to the house in the areas not lit by the IR cameras. I opened the door to side entrance room. I checked the trippers. The CCTV cameras were connected to a separate tripper, which was connected to a relay that was connected to a dedicated battery generator. Usually, they connect the tripper to the battery generator and the battery generator to the line. They may have added this relay to obfuscate the connections. I went back up the pole and restored the electricity.

My third trip coincided with their town's foundation day. I was going to grab the dark girl's partner this time. The dogs were going to be a problem. Ordinarily, I would have attacked the dogs but Zuma prohibited that. Most guard dogs are trained not to eat unauthorized foods so it was pointless to dope them or poison them. This country has laws against cruelty to animals, says Zuma. This country has too many laws, says me.

En route to my destination, I checked several pounds and finally found a bitch in heat. I observed the property all day with the drone. In the evening, the family left for the town in a car. However, they let the dogs loose on the property. Just before sundown, I attracted the dogs' attention using a dog whistle. When they reached the fence, they became overcome with frenzy. I muzzled the bitch and tied it to a tree some distance away from the fence and down the hillside. I then shot tranquilizer darts on the guard dogs. For extra safety, I muzzled them and tied their legs with some paracord that I had in my bag. I then climbed the street pole and disconnected the power supply.

I ate some chocolate bars while I waited for around a quarter of an hour. I noticed no movement in the house. I crossed the fence and moved to the side entrance where the IR lights were not shining. I jimmied the door latch with my crowbar and entered the mains room. I switched off all the trippers. I switched off all the generators. I used my night-vision camera to the check the CCTV cameras. They seemed to have turned off. Just then, a door opened. A burly man calmly walked in and switched on an emergency lamp on the wall. He nodded to me and with a smile locked the door behind him. He was barrel-chested. His shoulders were broad like that of a gorilla. He removed his coat and dropped it on the floor. He removed his holster and dropped it over the coat. Next, he walked over to the outside door and bolted it. He then raised his hands and beckoned me for a fight.

The lockdown has given rise to so many casual criminals that the public has lost fear of real decent hardworking criminals. (I may have come from another country but I am only committing crimes that the local criminals do not want to do.) The sudden appearance of the man should have made me soil my pants. For some strange reason, I was overcome with relief that there was just this one guy and no more dogs. Uncertainty is a bitch.

I removed my bag and placed it on a generator. I placed my crowbar on the bag and I invited the man for a fight in exactly the same manner as he did.

'Fight' is not the right word to describe it. It was more of a scuffle. It lasted only a minute. Initially, the man made some wrestling manoeuvres. I wasn't going to wrestle with this neanderthal. He charged forward and I side-stepped him. He was not so nimble because of his weight. I did not try to punch him. Punches would have had no impact because he had slit-like eyes, a small nose and almost non-existent lips. It was as if his mother had dropped him on his face when he was a child. I tried to choke him from behind but he threw me overhead. I landed on all fours in front of him. I saw him back up and then run forward to kick me. I avoided him just in time. I then drop-kicked him on his head. He staggered back, slipped and hit hard on the window grill. The sound resonated for a few seconds. He brought down a lot of curtains. And then, it was curtains for him.

I tore up some curtain cloth and stuffed his mouth with it. Then, I gagged him. I tied his hands and feet behind him with some paracord.

Grabbing the snake was much easier and less eventful. I broke the lock and noticed some motion detectors. These were battery-powered and switched on when I entered. They however could not raise an alarm. I found the snake easily as it was the only animal in the zoo. I put on another mask and a set of goggles as I did not want the poison enter my eyes or fall on my face. I put on my voltage-rated gloves and grabbed the snake by its head. The reptile coiled around my leg. I held a sack in front of the snake and drew the snake's head into it. After some reluctance, it darted into the sack. If it hadn't, I would have given it some motivation using an acetylene torch that I had with me. The reason why the owner wanted the snake was clear by now. This specimen was much longer than the average length that copperheads grow in the wild.

"What happened to the dog?"

"I removed its tag and left it at another shelter. What are you going to do with the snake?"

"What else? I'm going to reunite it with its partner."

"Can I come and see it?"

"You want to look at the girl, don't you?"

"Can I?"

"No."

I went outside and sat in my chair. Sometime later, I saw two snakes crawl out of the window in Zuma's room. Zuma came back after a while.

"What did they say?"

"They said you are dangerous."

"Two snakes said I'm dangerous?"

"They kill only for food. You kill because you hate."

"I should have taken them to a Chinese restaurant."

The Haunting

This new client refused to tell who referred him to me. When someone is stingy with important details like that, I refuse to work. However, he was generous with the purse upfront. That changed everything. I maybe a coward but as Daffy Duck would say I am a greedy little coward. I just need to be more careful. That's all.

This man had bought a property in a neighbouring state some years ago. He had bought the place because of the unbelievably low price the owners had offered it for, and for the peace and quiet. It was on the outer limits of a rather isolated coastal town. However, it was very close to the highway that linked the town to the outside world. It was far away from the beach so very few people even knew that it existed. His family complained of uneasiness during the day and sleeplessness during the night while they stayed there. Later, he learned from someone in town that the house and the grounds it stood in was known to be haunted. The property has been bought several times in the last few decades. A family would move in, live a few years and then quit. The house had remained unoccupied most of the time.

The man's personal details checked out. He was who he claimed he was. There seemed nothing averse to investigating the case.

I took keys to the property from the man and rode a rental motorcycle to the place. The plot was so large that I could not see the fence in any direction. The house was big and had two floors. There was a basement below the main hall, library, dining room, store room and kitchen. There were some recent footprints in the basement so I decided not to do any further exploration. The house was in good condition even though it was over 100 years old. There were trees all over the plot but for some space around the house the ground had been cleared for maintaining a lawn. There was even a pond with an artificial fountain. The water storage at the top of the house was clean.

Inside the house, the rooms were big but not as many I thought there would be. I wondered why anyone would want to sleep in such a large bedroom. There were two wings from main portion with just three rooms in each. The house had accumulated a lot of furniture and carpeting over the years.

I checked all the rooms for safety hazards. I found none. I checked the plumbing, doors and windows. I could find no hidden contraptions. I scanned for radio transmissions of audio beeps. I checked for infra-red lighting in the dark. Nothing. The walls were very high so I couldn't check everywhere.

I spent the night in the upper floor in one of the corner bedrooms. It had a new bed. I had a strange dream that night. I was back in my teen years and was walking home from the main bus stand of my hometown. Some adult acquaintance was walking with me. I am unable to recall who it was. A tall woman intercepted me and said, "Shall we go?" I then excused myself from the acquaintance and followed the woman. She walked in front of me and I meekly followed her. She did not say anything and I did not try to talk to her. Eventually, she reached a lake. Most of my class friends lived on the other side of the lake. Just me and two other guys lived on this side of the lake. She stopped at a tiny isolated thatch-roofed house on the embankment. She opened the door and invited me in as she went in. She then disappeared into the darkness inside. I did not know if I should follow her and hesitated. I turned to see if I could just quietly leave without telling her. Whatever I saw behind me horrified and startled me that I opened the door and went in. Inside the house, I fell on the floor and it was all dark again. Suddenly, a light appeared. I saw the whole lake above me. I saw the clouds and the sun shining through the water. I was afraid I was going to drown even though the water did not touch me. I was cold all over and could not move. I struggled but it was like I was tied up with ropes. I then woke up and realised it was all a dream.

My LED lamp was where I had left it. It was on the floor under the bed. It lit up the whole room in an eerie but effective sort of way. One of the windows was open and my sheet was off. Everything was cold to touch. I closed the window. I went to pee and returned to bed. That was it. No ghosts or whatever.

The next day, I went to the town's main street and bought some work supplies. I hired an electrician there. He was available for only a few hours. At the house, we both checked all the circuits and could not find anything wrong. The previous owners had complained that they had heard weird noises and strange unexplained movements of furniture. I thought these were just mechanical or electronic contraptions designed to scare the occupants. Who was trying to scare them and why?

While the guy was working, I marked some furniture as too old and troublesome. I took them out one by one and burned them with a flame thrower. The only part of the house that remained to be inspected was the basement.

In the afternoon, the electrician discovered something strange. He could not trace a few lines in the ground floor. In one of the rooms, the lines did not pass over to the next room and they were not going into the room either. I then discovered that the lengths of the inside walls did not match with the outside wall. There was a diffrence of three feet. The wall between the two rooms could not be that thick. I drilled a hole in the outside wall and there was indeed an enclosed room between the two rooms. I asked the electrician to come the next day so that we could both check the basement. We then left for town. I had my lunch there.

Back at the house, I found an old car parked in the front. Inside the car, it smelled of turpentine. I found the reason. There was a tightly bound bundle of sachets containing some white powder.

I heard some signs of human presence from the basement. There, I found a bunch of guys sitting in a circle. One of them stood up but the rest of them paid no attention to me. They had spread some pieces of newspapers and had a lit candle in the middle. I asked them what they were doing there but they pretended like I was invisible. I raised my foot and pushed one of the men on the head. He hit the candle and fell on the papers. Suddenly, all of them acted on a common stimuli and seemed to finally acknowledge my presence. The guy who stood up took out a knife and asked me to get out if I wanted to live. I raised my hands in peace and walked back. I returned with the flame thrower and set the men on fire. They were five of them and they all ran out. Some of them yelled threats as they bundled into their car and left.

I got my motorcycle out of its hiding place. Don't blame me. This has become a habit. I followed the car to town where they stopped at a pharmacy. They then drove to a deli. After some discussion in the parking lot, all of them went in.

I put on my hood and shades. I made an anonymous phone call from a pay phone. (It was the only one in the town and very old, I was told.) I am not yet a citizen but I care about the society I live in. About ten minutes later, a plainclothesman inspected the car. He then went to a car parked on the road and took out a shotgun. A uniformed man with another shotgun stepped out of the vehicle. They both went inside the deli. I had asked them not to sound their sirens so this was all according to plan. The gang members trooped out with their hands held behind their heads. The gang leader stepped out of line, ran over to his car and sped away. The plainclothesman shot at his feet and then at his car.

I then went over to the pay phone to make another anonymous phone call to the Sheriff's office. This time, I got there without the hood or the shades. Unfortunately, I did not have any more coins to make the call. I took out my mobile phone, placed it next to the mouthpiece of the pay phone and pressed a few numbers. I cannot say what those numbers were but it made the payphone's display change from 'Drop coin' to 'Dial number'. I am surprised the hack continues to work after so many decades of being discovered! When I got connected, I congratulated the police force for being such a useless bunch of nincompoops. I care about society but I am also a critic.

I chipped the hole large enough to shine a torch inside it. There was a secret room all right but there was nothing in it. There was some packaging cardboard on the floor and I assumed that it covered an entrance into the basement. However, the basement that I saw earlier was much smaller and did not extend all the way to this room. This meant that there was another basement room that was connected or not connected to the main one in the middle of the house. I then demolished part of the wall so that I could let myself in. I had to work slowly for a few hours because I did not want to cause collateral damage with my hammer. I did not have my takeout dinner until I was finished with the wall. I decided to take some rest before I went down to the basement through secret entrance. Unfortunately, I fell asleep on the bed.

I dreamt that I was lying on a forest floor and wolves were eating my body. I could not move or shoo them away. My body seemed paralysed and I woke up after a long struggle. It was midnight. A window was open and everything was cold to touch. Did I forget to close it? Was it the ghost? I was annoyed like hell.

I pondered over whether I should be investigating the basement room in the middle of the night. The chicken in me said, 'Forget it!'. The curious cat in me said, 'Go and solve the mystery.' When this is over, I should go to a doctor and get them both euthanised. I took my crowbar and the lamp and walked over to the demolished wall.

I climbed inside the secret room. When I removed cardboard, a plastic sheet underneath it just collapsed and fell into the basement below. There was a flight of steps. If the steps were made of wood, I told myself, I am not going to down there. The steps could break and I could hurt myself. Or, a putrefied demon, like the one from the movie *Evil Dead*, might stalk me and grab me from behind. I will wait for the next day and let some professionals do the investigation.

Unfortunately, the steps were solid, built with brick and mortar. There was no turning back now. The steps led to the basement floor. It was covered in places with some black material, which I assumed was wall rot. There must have been some moisture ingress in some years. Everything was dry now and there was no chance I would slip on the floor. There was nothing in the room except for an old wooden bureau and a freezer. There were some old table cloth and bathroom towels in the bureau. I opened the freezer and found a human skeleton. I did not have to double-check it to see if it was a pig or the leg of a cow. It was a human all right. The room was flooded with the smell of old leather and dried fish. I could not stand there. I left as quickly as I could. I grabbed the plastic sheet and walked up the steps. I spread it over the entrance and placed the cardboard pieces over it.

I went back to my room and washed my face. I could still smell the skeleton. I took a shower and took special care to wash my nostrils. Back in my room, I applied some *javadu* powder to my chest. The odour was gone but my lungs still felt strange.

I went to sleep again but woke up when I thought I heard something. I got up and put the pillows under my sheet. I then grabbed my crowbar and hid next to the door. A few minutes later, the door knob turned. Someone opened the door and entered the room. It was the leader of the junkie gang. I drove the crowbar into his chest and punched his face. He was out. I went out of the room and then checked the stairs. There was no one. I looked out of the window and their car was parked in the front of the house! I went back to my room and grabbed my machete from the bag. I then dragged the gang leader out and threw him down the stairs. Nothing happened. No one came to his rescue. I went out of the house and checked the car. I then broke all the windows and windshields on the car. Their contraband was still in it. I am not telling the police again. I will just inform the owner what happened and let him figure it out. I am out of here. I let the air out of the wheels. I turned to get my stuff from the house and stood facing the gang leader again. He had a gun and it was pointed at me. I should have tied him up. When anger comes in, thinking goes out.

The next day was unremarkable except that I had to pee in my pants a few times. The gang leader had tied me to a sofa in the main hall and did not bother me after that. On the second day of my captivity, I woke up to the sounds of birds and an explosion. During the previous night, I dreamt of Zuma. She asked me if I was all right. I could not say anything as I was gagged, even in the dream. I had placed a short-wave beacon in the motorcycle. Like the lamp, I had built the beacon myself. It is designed to send regular SOS signals if it was not reset in the morning. The receiver was in my house. I wondered if it picked up the SOS and raised an alarm. I did not have time to test it at long distances. You go to war with whatever you have.

The explosion blew up several window panes and few glass pieces landed next to me. I picked one with my feet and cut the ropes. The gang leader came out with his gun and found that their car had blown up. He was soon met with a hail of gunfire. Who was this? The pigs? A rival gang? After a while, it was clear that there was just one shooter and he was using an automatic weapon. The gang leader was firing from the upper floor. From the sounds of it, he tried different locations but his shots were useless. I think he had a handgun and a shotgun. The outside shooter had a rifle and had better range. After some time, he switched from automatic to semi-automatic fire. It was clear that he was running low on ammunition. Finally, I got free from the ropes. My feet hurt and I was weak with hunger. I had to act as it was now or never. I drank some water from a bottle of water that I had left there. My body absorbed the water like a sponge. I felt like a new man. I went to the upper floor as stealthily as I could. I found the gang leader using binoculars to spot the shooter. When he backed up after an exchange of fire, I … I cannot say what I did but with timely medical care, he might live.

I then took his shotgun and ammo, and went downstairs. The confrontation took the breath out of me and I was feeling weak again. I went down to the kitchen and drank some more water. I went out of the house through the kitchen backdoor. I approached the location of the shooter in a roundabout way. It was Zuma. She was firing from behind the trees. She had a hunting rifle with a sight and a Kalashnikov. I don't know where she got them. She was wearing an outfit quite different from her regular work clothes. I leaned the shotgun on a tree. I then approached Zuma with my hands in the air in a non-threatening manner.

My beacon does not function at great distances. Zuma refused to tell me why or how she showed up like she did. I have my secrets and she has hers. I told my client that his property was unlikely to have ghosts now. To be sure, I asked him to get the skeleton released and arrange a proper religious burial. The pigs identified the dead person as a woman who worked for one of the previous owners. When this owner died, she left the property to her two servants. One of them killed the other and lived in the house for a decade with the body still in the freezer. Eventually, he decided to sell out and move to a different state. That was when he built a wall to cover up what was just a small corridor. The second basement had existed before his time. He now lives in New Zealand where he had bought a farm. Efforts are on to extradite him. The pigs also found some weapons and a lot of contraband in the main basement. The drug gang has been using the place for a few weeks. The gang leader is still in hospital. The pigs took away Zuma's rifles. They said she will have to sue the state if she wanted them back. Zuma not only sued the state but also forced them to settle. She received legal aid from a gun club and the case received an expedited hearing. The state settled because they did not want to pay damages.

Family Planning

Next morning, I started feeling miserable. We will have to say our goodbyes in the evening. I felt like a kid who could not enjoy his Sunday because next day was Monday. Should I pop the question? If not, I may not see her again.

"Are you planning to get these stories published?"

"Maybe someday."

Silence.

"I spoke to your friend about you. She confirms that you are single."

"It is true."

"Do you plan to get married?"

"Someday."

"Do you have any candidates lined up?"

"No."

"Can you put me on the list?"

"Are you interested?"

"Yes."

"What make you think you might be the ideal candidate?"

"I'm the ideal candidate for any girl. You cannot go wrong with me. Your friend already made all the matching and crossing."

"She does that all the time."

"So, you are not interested?"

"I'm not sure if you are serious."

"I have been serious about getting married ever since I was a little kid. I did not have any money then. Now, I have money. I'm tired of living alone. Cooking for one person is really terrible."

"So, you want someone who will cook for you?"

"That and other things."

We laughed.

"If you don't know, I can teach you."

"What?"

"Cooking."

"You seem convinced that it is the wife's job to cook."

"I have written a nice story about it. Would you like to hear it?"

"Sure."

In prehistoric times, early man and woman were equals. Or, nobody gave it a thought. Because of superior physical strength, men became hunters. Women became gatherers. But, they both had to work all day to fend for themselves and their families. One day, a woman discovered that food cooked on fire tasted better. She taught other women how to create fire and use it for cooking food and for heating the dwelling place. The stupid men were afraid of the fire. They liked the food and the warmth of the fire but did not want to deal with it directly. So, the women decided to take advantage of the situation. They offered to stay at home and mind the fire and do household chores while the menfolk went out and brought the food. Thus, for thousands of years, the matriarchy exploited men. Women would do the cooking, clean the house and mind the children. This left them with a lot of free time to while away. Their lot was better than that of men because the latter had to till the ground, raise the animals, build roads, transport goods, pay taxes, fight wars, etc. With industrialization and urbanization, possession of money (rather than manual labour) mattered more. Many men's jobs had became tied to sitting in a cushy chair. They worked in air-conditioned offices and enjoyed many perks, instead of having to toil on the factory floor or dig dirt in a coal mine. Men were now seemingly having a good time while women thought they were slaving over a hot stove all day. Women became jealous and wanted to leave the kitchen. And, many of them did. Of course, they were paid a lot less and had to make more sacrifices than men. They still considered themselves liberated -- from the kitchen, that is.

"A likely story."

"Will you or will you not marry me?"

"A lot of guys say they want to marry just to get into a girl's pants."

"So, you think this is just a drama?"

"Many women have been fooled by marriage talk."

"You are wrong. No man had ever fooled a woman with an offer of marriage. The women were so horny themselves that they decided to lower their standards, just like the men. I just want you to say okay to our marriage before we leave today. I have no other plans."

"So, do you love me?"

"I can't answer that until we get married. I don't fool around with women. I don't want say 'I love you' to someone if there is no prospect of getting married. If you marry me, I will love you."

She was thinking.

"Okay. Let us say we wait another month. And, if you are still interested and this is not some ruse, we will get married."

"Really? One month and we get married?

She nodded.

"Fine by me. Hey, let's go and buy some ice cream… to celebrate."

"I'm also coming."

"Me too."

"What are you guys doing here? When did they get here?"

"A few moments ago."

"All right. Let's go."

"So, you think it is always a woman's fault if she gets pregnant?"

"There are guys who rape or spike a woman's drink. Then, it is not her fault. If she says she was fooled by an offer of marriage, it is definitely her fault. Besides that, a pregnancy can be easily avoided even after the act."

"How?"

"If a woman has done things unprotected, she can still visit a gynæcologist and get a copper IUD inserted. An intra-uterine device is a metallic thingy that will physically obstruct a fertilized egg from attaching to the uterus and becoming a baby. It should be done within a few days after the event."

"How do you know this information?"

"Some years ago, there was a big controversy about a hormonal drug for woman and a gynæcologist wrote an article saying that when there were simple mechanical contraception contraptions, there was no need to use chemicals to alter the hormones in the body of a woman. Hormones control several known and unknown functions in the body. Messing up with that is not safe. Do you think men will ever take hormones? Why are women so willing to take this risk? In that article, she mentioned this stuff about copper IUDs."

"Even I don't know this."

"A woman has to remain chaste only for a few days around the mid-portion of her menstrual cycle and she will not pregnant. In the beginning of the cycle, the egg cannot get fertilized because it is not in the proper location and the conditions are unfavourable. In the latter part of the cycle, the unfertilized and unattached egg gets auto-destroyed and flushed out. So, there are several days in a month when it is safe, that is, if her cycles are regular and predictable."

"How do you know these things?"

"I wanted to be a doctor. That is why I chose the science group in higher-secondary. I was weak in maths and did not pass the entrance exam. I'm a clean freak now. I would not have survived as a doctor. I'm happy I failed. A doctor's job is disgusting."

On the way to the shop, the girl kid asked, "Do you think my father is goofy?"

"No, that is an exaggeration. We have studied in the same school ever since we were three years old. We can say whatever we want. It means nothing."

She did not seem convinced.

"Your father did better than me. He got a job before I did. He got married before I did. He got a house before I did."

Vampira tapped my shoulder.

"Tell me, why should I marry you?"

"Because I'm the handsomest guy anywhere and if there are any other pretenders they are just goofy."

"Being handsome — that's the only reason?"

"What else is there? You don't want ugly kids, do you? Don't look at them. They are lucky they got their looks from their mother. You can't take risks with genetic lottery. Tell me, honey, do you have any exciting offers from anyone else other than me?"

"Honey?" It was the girl.

"No, just you, sweetheart."

"Sweetheart?" It was the boy.

"Well, kids, we are in love."

"This love fest makes me wanna puke!" Then, he proceeded to have a seizure, fell down and started convulsing. He must have learned that line from some TV programme.

"You cannot have an epileptic attack and also be vomiting. The two symptoms are contradictory."

"Tell me... when you asked me to marry you, was that just a spur-of-the-moment thing or was there some real thought given to it?"

"I've told you. I've been wanting to get married for a long time. I had a lot of trouble finding the right girl."

"So, I'm the right one?"

"No, I wanted to marry some film actresses but I would never have the courage to speak to them. You... I can speak to." I went to pay for the ice cream.

"Should I take that as a compliment?" she yelled. I gestured her to hold for a moment while I got the goodies.

I gave her her cone.

"There are plenty of girls who are pretty. Thin and pretty... very difficult to find. Women swell up like a blimp after they get married so it is important to start from a small footprint. Besides, you are not wearing any makeup. Natural beauties are impossible to find in the wild. Do you know how many tons of wax and paint women put on their faces each year? I once saw a video of a woman who was reviewing several things she had in her bag. She had some feel-good excuse for every item. 'This one is made by indigenous tribes'. 'That one has been tested on cruelty-free chicken.'"

"Why are you watching makeup videos? These are videos BY women and FOR women."

I thought for a while. "I don't know. One thing..."

"... led to another," she finished my sentence.

"I saw some non-makeup-related video of hers and decided to check what else she had. There was a lot of makeup videos with titles I did not understand. This video had a title I did understand."

"'Things I have in my handbag'? What do you care what women have in their handbag?"

"I see a lot of survival videos and EDC or Every Day Carry is a popular topic."

“Proceed.”

“You don’t think…”

“No.”

“You don’t think what no?”

“Nothing.”

“You know when couples tend to evaluate their mates under a microscope, they end up missing the forest for the trees. Any couple, whatever the flaws, can be happy if both partners try to make the other one happy.”

Silence.

“Anyway, every product she reviewed had some phony justification. She did not buy something simply because it was good. It had to have a sob story attached to it. These women care so much about the environment and talk about reducing their carbon footprint all the time. Do they know how much carbon is in the wax and paint they are putting on their faces? She mentioned something called ‘foundation’. It sounds just like the primer used to paint walls!”

“Never mind all that. Return to subject. You decided to marry me because I’m thin, pretty and wear no makeup?”

“People fall in love for no reason. I cannot explain my decision. My mind was made up yesterday. I asked myself if I had made the right choice. Thin and pretty tilted the scale. I don’t care for the environment. Just marry me. I’m sure I can make any woman happy.”

“Okay. I believe you but don’t test on any other woman.”

“Will do.”

“Don’t do!”

“All right.”

She thought for a while. “And, I cannot wear makeup?”

“Wear makeup if you want. Don’t wear it all day or every day. I don’t think the stuff is healthy. Everything you put on your face gets into the blood… I think. When I was a kid, I saw a video of an actress demonstrating her makeup process.”

“Here we go again!”

What’s her problem? “In those days, we had only two channels and we saw every program we could. Do you want the story or not?… Well, she was already very pretty. She did a lot of drawing, shading, painting, buffing, sprinkling… But, at the end, she was several times prettier than in the beginning! Her face was like a painting. It was magical. Makeup can be like a magic spell. That is why I do not trust women wearing makeup. For all you know, there might be some hideous monster hiding under those layers of coat and varnish.”

“Give women some credit. There could be a monster behind a naturally pretty face too.”

“That’s fine. I’m superficial. I don’t care for the brains.”

“You care only for the brawn?”

“I care for beauty — natural beauty.”

“Oh, shut up.”

We got married next month. My friend stopped making four-legged jokes and so did I. We rented the same cottage for our honeymoon even though it was raining heavily. We felt lonely inside the place. We called our friends and spent another happy weekend together with them.

“When are they coming?”

“They will be here tomorrow morning and we can all leave together on the day after in the evening.”

“So, today is going to be one long extremely boring day.”

“I wrote something this morning based on yesterday's events. Would you like to hear it?”

“Anything.”

“It is called ‘Sam & Saw’.”

“Why ‘Sam & Saw’?”

“It stands for *Stone Age Man & Stone Age Woman. SAM & SAW*”

“Go ahead with it.”

One day, SAM proposed marriage to SAW. SAW accepted the offer and married SAM. They got married because it was customary. They did not know anything about being a man and wife. They just lived together. One day, it rained and they got wet.

SAM said, "Let's go and hide in that cave where they store the leather."

After the reached the cave, SAM made a bed out of the leatherskins while SAW swept the floor.

"Cooking, cleaning and washing. Forever, the woman's duties."

"Don't get ahead of the story."

"I hate the story already."

"Please!"

"All right. Finish it quick."

"Why? Do you have anything else in mind?"

"No."

"All right."

SAW hung her clothes on the line. When she turned, she noticed something odd.

"Why is there a bulge in your pocket every time I take off my coconut shells?

Vampira threw a pillow at me.

"Take off your pants. Let's see what's under there."

SAM protested in vain.

"What the heck is that? Is it a snake? What are you doing with it? Here, let me kill it."

Vampira picked up another pillow and started hitting me with it. I slipped from the bed to the floor and continued reading in upside-down position.

She tried to take the knife from his belt but SAM held her at bay. "Stop it! Don't do anything rash. It is nothing to be afraid off. It is a part of me. Just don't bother about it."

"Well, your snake has sprayed its poison everywhere. I just swept the place."

Vampira tried to kill a laugh and failed.

"Why do you have it? What if it bites YOU?"

Vampira laughed without any restraint for a whole minute. After that, she refused to look at me. She stared at the ceiling and begged, "Stop it! Stop it! Stop it!"

SAM then whispered in her ear that as his legal wife she

was duty-bound to cover it with the hole she had in the same place on her body.

"I won't even live with you if you harbour that poisonous creature. I say we cut it off and throw it in the garbage. Maybe some bird will come and eat it."

After a lot of effort, SAM convinced SAW that there was no need to overreact. After a few months of experimentation, SAW became pregnant.

"I should have killed that snake when I had the chance. Now, I have a big bulge and it is much much bigger than his," SAW told her mother.

Several months later, a baby was born. Next year, it rained and the inevitable happened. Another baby. This time, however, SAW had stitched a leather rain coat for him.

"I don't need it. If you wear it, this thing won't happen again."

"End of story."

"I should have never married a writer."

Well, you have finished the book. If you give it a good review or rating (☆ ☆ ☆ ☆ ☆) online, it would be much appreciated. If you have any corrections or suggestions, write to me at Info@VSubhash.Com.

I have written more than two dozen non-fiction books on a wide range of subjects. Some of them are available for FREE on several ebook stores and library apps. Check the backlist for more details or visit: www.VSubhash.IN/books.html

Books By V. Subhash

I invite you to visit my site **WWW.VSUBHASH.IN**, and check out my other books, special discounts, sample PDFs and full ebooks. In 2020, I started publishing books. For two decades before that, I have been publishing feature articles, free ebooks (old editions still available), software (server/desktop/mobile), reviews (books, films, music and travel), funny memes and cartoons. My books for children are under the pseudonym **Ólafía L. Óla** (because it has laugh and LOL).

2020 Fresh Clean Jokes For Everyone

This is one of the biggest jokebooks ever written - over 3200 jokes spread over:

- *Part 1 — For Learning* (computer jokes, programming jokes, physics jokes, chemistry jokes, biology jokes, medical jokes, financial jokes, geography jokes, pun jokes and THREE CHAPTERS DEVOTED TO FOREIGN LANGUAGES)
- *Part 2 — For Fun* (bar jokes, blonde jokes, cross-the-road jokes, knock-knock jokes, lightbulb jokes, knock-knock jokes, romantic (breakup) jokes)
- *Part 3 — Only For Intellectuals* (jokes about philosophy, advertising, news and politics)

It has lots of jokes purely for the hedonist consumption of humour, content to improve vocabulary and general knowledge, thought-provoking poems (mostly as financial/political limericks set to the tune of popular nursery rhymes) AND some of the best one-liners EVER written in English. Absolutely no (x) humour.

• Pages: 292   • Paperback: $10   • Ebook: An older subset with 420 jokes is available FOR FREE

2020 Fresh Clean Jokes For Kids

This 'for kids' subset of the 2020 jokebook has over 2200 jokes. It has all of *Part 1 (For Learning)* and some non-political jokes from *Part 2 (For Fun)* & *Part 3 (Only For Intellectuals)*. Joke types include computer jokes, programming jokes, cross-the-road jokes, physics jokes, chemistry jokes, biology jokes, medical jokes, financial jokes, geography jokes, knock-knock jokes, breakup jokes...). Special chapters include *Elephant & Ant Jokes*, *Off-The-Wall Philosophers*, *Useful French Phrases*, *Useful Latin Phrases*, *Other Useful Foreign Phrases*, *Jokes You Love To Hate*, *Jokes In Advertising*, and *Fancy Creature Jokes*. No political or controversial jokes. Absolutely no (x) humour.

• Pages: 166   • Paperback: ₹550 or $7.70   • Ebook: Will never be published

World of Word Ladders

Word ladders puzzles have the right balance between exercising the brain and having fun. A word ladder has a diagram of a ladder with a word on both the first and last rungs. You need to change only one letter in the blank middle rungs so that the first word is transformed into the last word.

The solutions in this book are obscured to retain the challenge.

Here are two examples of word ladders:

- **C-A-T** » *C-O-T* » *C-O-D* » *C-O-G* » **D-O-G**
- **L-A-S-T** » *L-O-S-T* » *L-O-S-E* » *H-O-S-E* » **H-O-P-E**

• Puzzles: 100   • Paperback: $6 (per volume)

Unlikely Stories

This is a full-colour illustrated anthology of horror & comedy stories — an exorcism, an alien encounter, a haunted lift, a seance, a shapeshifter, a werewolf, a talking bird, an evil twin, an alien invasion and a distressed alpaca — all wrapped in a very witty love story. The author originally intended to write a non-fiction book based on real-life incidents. He was however **forced by several governments** to name this book as '*Unlikely Stories*' and release it only as a fiction title. The stories have turned out to be **supernatural/paranormal/sci-fi fantasies with ample doses of action, horror and humour**. The entire book is in first person and everything happens very fast. There is never a dull moment.

First edition stories

- **The trip**: The lead is invited by his friend to a resort where he meets the first heroine *Vampira*.
- **The swim**: The lead decides that Vampira is his soul mate he has been waiting all his life. He tells several stories to entertain his friend's kids and also impress Vampira.
- **The exorcist**: The second lead is an Indian crook who escapes to the West to start a new life. He attempts to go legit but finds competition from a professional medium operating under the trade name of *Mademoiselle Zuma*. She is dangerous because she is a mind-reader.
- **Alien encounter**: After the successful exorcism, this lead is asked to help a teenager who has been repeatedly 'abducted' by an alien.
- **The lift**: A recently deceased security guard haunts a lift where he had died and seeks revenge.
- **Femme fatale**: The second lead has a showdown with a female animal spirit.

- **The seance**: A young woman in the city is troubled by nightmares involving a hooded skeleton. A newly married nurse blanks out every night. She is also troubled by bizarre nightmares. Mademoiselle Zuma solves both cases.
- **The haunting**: An old mansion is haunted by a presence. Every new buyer and his family gets driven to such desperation that they eventually sell. The second lead investigates and almost gets killed.
- **Family planning**: The first lead and Vampira plan their life together. In the first ending, they get married. In the second ending (written by the lead after their first night), **Stone Age Man (SAM)** and **Stone Age Woman (SAW)** discover the mystery of life. (This is an over-the-top parody of the **controversy about *MEN WRITING WOMEN***.) Other than some intimate events implied in comic fashion, there is no physical contact between the sexes in the entire book. Not even a kiss. The book is clean throughout. No swear words. No corny mushy dialogue. No degeneracy. No weirdness. Just no low-hanging fruit.

Second edition stories (*Mademoiselle Zuma Chronicles*)

- **Shadows in the night**: A young woman is troubled by a ghostly intruder at night.
- **Zuma vs. Cutie**: Zuma finds competition from an unlikely friend.
- **The evil twin**: A rich heiress is driven to desperation by a deceased twin who wants her to die as well.

- **The alien invasion**: A bolide crashes down in the Atlantic. The site becomes an alien platform for launching attacks on English-speaking countries. No other countries are attacked. The world's sole super power collapses after a few days. The strangest thing about the invasion is that the aliens' primary objective is not humans but cows. This is no run-of-the-mill alien invasion story. Uniquely, it provides an fascinating economic model for staging a successful alien invasion.
- **Please do not smile at our alpaca**: Zuma and her husband restart a farm devastated by the aliens. Things go well until her husband picks a fight with a South American.

NOTE: This second edition is a FULL-COLOUR illustrated book with several new stories written from the perspective of Zuma.

• 1st edition paperback (140 small grayscale-illustrated pages): $9   • 2nd edition paperback (122 bigger colour-illustrated pages): $16   • 1st edition ebook: ₹100 • 2nd edition ebook: ₹200

How To Invest In Stocks, 2nd Edition

The first edition book was written in 2003 for the Indian stockmarket. It was popular around the world because it was a plain-English guide to investing in the stockmarket. The 2020 completely revised second edition maintains the original premise but has a global focus, updated information and new chapters. **It has some useful 'extra' information that you will not find in any investment book and no business school will teach you.** Mere book knowledge about stockmarkets will not help you understand the markets. Markets are influenced by news and information (there is a difference).

- Pages: 94   • Paperback: $9.90   • Ebook: ₹100 or FREE

Learn To Ride A Motorcycle In Five Minutes

Yes, you can! For most of my life, I did not know how to ride a motorbike. But, when I had to do, it took me only five minutes. On my first ride on my first bike, I travelled nearly 100 kilometres, across two cities and one national highway. Acquiring the skill takes less than five minutes and honing it will require a few weeks.

- Pages: 40 (30 with real content)   • Paperback: $7.70
- Ebook: ₹100, $6

How To Install Solar

This is a heavily illustrated guidebook for **INDIAN** solar power enthusiasts, DIY hacks, home-owners and electricians about solar panels, batteries, inverters, charge controllers, installation procedures and costs. It starts with a simple introduction to home electrical systems, proceeds on to describe various aspects of solar power and options available for home owners, and then provides step-by-step instructions for installing a low-cost DC-only solar charge controller system for ₹6000

and a solar inverter system providing AC power backup for ₹30,000. Also included is an extensive FAQs section based on questions and reviews published by solar power users online.

- Pages: 76   • Colour paperback: $7.70   • Ebook: ₹100

Cool Electronic Projects

If you are learning electronics or thinking of it as a future hobby, this FULL-COLOUR book has some fun projects to begin with. They will not waste your time or money, will be extremely useful (particularly in emergencies) and are quite easy to make. Just one of these projects uses AC (alternating current). The rest work on DC (direct current) and are safe for kids (if you think soldering is safe). These projects are good for the environment too, as they reuse electronic parts that would have been discarded. If you are a survivalist, then you will be happy that all the projects will run off-the-grid, as they can consume renewable energy. For the tinkerer, there are projects that add MORE POWER than what the manufacturer had provided. For the parent of lazy children, there are annoying alarms that can wake up the dead.

• Pages: 40 (33 with real content)   • Paperback: $9.90   • Ebook: ₹100

PC Hardware Explained

You can build a PC in 30 minutes with just a screwdriver. Knowing which computer components will work together is not so easy. This full-colour paperback will explain computer hardware using **simple terms, illustrations, photographs and tables**. Before **buying a new laptop from the store** or **assembling a new desktop from parts**, get this book. You will be able to read the technical specifications of a PC and understand what it can and cannot do. The mumbo-jumbo in the sales pitch of a new computer will be understandable.

• Pages: 30 (22 with real content)   • Colour paperback: $7   • Ebook: ₹100

CommonMark Ready Reference

MarkDown is an easy human-readable text format that can serve as the common base for exporting to multiple document formats such as HTML, ODF, DOC/DOCX, PDF and ebook (EPUB, MOBI…). It is a great tool for authors, technical writers and content developers to create books, manuals, web pages and other rich-text content. CommonMark is a new well-formed standard for the old MarkDown spec. **CommonMark was one of the reasons I was able to write and design 21 books in one year.** Incidentally, this is the first-ever book on CommonMark. You will be buying a piece of history! This book's covers are designed like a quick reference card.

• Pages: 56 (39 with real content)   • Paperback: $7   • Ebook: ₹100 or FREE

Quick Start Guide to FFmpeg

- Need to process audio/video files without spending much on software?
- Need a quick tutorial or desk-side reference for FFmpeg?

FFmpeg is THE BEST software to easily create, edit, enhance and convert audio and video files. It is a FREE and open-source command-utility available for **Linux, Mac and Windows**. And, *Quick Start Guide to FFmpeg* is THE BEST book for an extensive FFmpeg tutorial, hack collection and quick reference. It is richly illustrated with color screenshots, code examples and tables to help you work with audio, video, images, animations, fonts, subtitles and metadata like a PRO. **NOTE**: The 2020 self-published book has been withdrawn. The new and updated book from Apress/SpringerNature was published in 2023.

• Pages: 280   • Colour Paperback: $44.99   • PDF Ebook: $29.99

Linux Command-Line Tips & Tricks

This is a tips-and-tricks collection for Linux command-line warriors. This book is at an advanced level. It assumes that you already know how to use the terminal and are adept at shell programming. It does not teach you the basics or try to be a comprehensive reference. It trusts your intuition and focuses on things you are most likely to forget. Because of its ancient history, BASH scripting has some odd programming constructs that are difficult to memorize. This  book tries to provide a ready-reference for such archaic but crucial details. The paperback has numerous screenshots and syntax-highlighted code examples, all in full-colour.

• Pages: 100   • Colour Paperback: $9.99   • Ebook: ₹100 or FREE

About the author

V. Subhash is an invisible Indian writer, programmer and cartoonist. Subhash pursues numerous hobbies and interests, several of which have become the subject of his books. In 2020, he published one of the biggest jokebooks of all time. Although he had published a few ebooks as early as 2003, Subhash did not publish traditional-style books until 2020. During this time, he had accumulated a lot of unpublished and published (**www.vsubhash.com**) material. This content and the automated book-production process that he had developed helped him publish 21 books in his first year. In February 2023, Apress (SpringerNature) published his rewritten and updated FFmpeg book as ***QUICK START GUIDE TO FFMPEG***. In 2022, Subhash ran out of non-fiction material and tried his hand at fiction. The result was ***UNLIKELY STORIES***, a collection of horror and comedy short stories.